"Suzy?"

Levi pushed back his Stetson and leaned close, looking straight into her eyes, his gaze compelling and demanding. Unyielding in a way she hadn't remembered.

And it was enough to pull her away from the edge, out of the panic.

"I'm fine."

He looked unconvinced, his brow furrowed, a five o'clock shadow giving him a tough edge that hadn't been there when they were kids. "Suzy–"

"Let's call it a day and say good-night."

Levi was still standing under the streetlight as she pulled out of the parking lot. The rose was on the ground beside him, a dark line on the pavement.

She hated roses.

She turned on the radio. Tomorrow would be another long day, and she needed to be ready for it.

Prayed she'd be ready for it.

TEXAS RANGER JUSTICE:
Keeping the Lone Star State safe

Daughter of Texas–Terri Reed, January 2011
Body of Evidence–Lenora Worth, February 2011
Face of Danger–Valerie Hansen, March 2011
Trail of Lies–Margaret Daley, April 2011
Threat of Exposure–Lynette Eason, May 2011
Out of Time–Shirlee McCoy, June 2011

Books by Shirlee McCoy

Love Inspired Suspense

Die Before Nightfall
Even in the Darkness
When Silence Falls
Little Girl Lost
Valley of Shadows
Stranger in the Shadows
Missing Persons
Lakeview Protector
**The Guardian's Mission*
**The Protector's Promise*
Cold Case Murder
**The Defender's Duty*
***Running for Cover*
Deadly Vows
***Running Scared*
***Running Blind*
Out of Time

*The Sinclair Brothers
**Heroes for Hire

Steeple Hill Trade

Still Waters

SHIRLEE McCOY

has always loved making up stories. As a child, she daydreamed elaborate tales in which she was the heroine—gutsy, strong and invincible. Though she soon grew out of her superhero fantasies, her love for storytelling never diminished. She knew early that she wanted to write inspirational fiction, and she began writing her first novel when she was a teenager. Still, it wasn't until her third son was born that she truly began pursuing her dream of being published. Three years later she sold her first book. Now a busy mother of five, Shirlee is a homeschool mom by day and an inspirational author by night. She and her husband and children live in Washington and share their house with a dog, two cats and a bird. You can visit her website at www.shirleemccoy.com, or email her at shirlee@shirleemccoy.com.

OUT OF TIME

SHIRLEE McCOY

Love Inspired

If you purchased this book without a cover you should be aware that this book is stolen property. It was reported as "unsold and destroyed" to the publisher, and neither the author nor the publisher has received any payment for this "stripped book."

Special thanks and acknowledgment to Shirlee McCoy
for her contribution
to the Texas Ranger Justice miniseries.

Recycling programs for this product may not exist in your area.

™ LOVE INSPIRED BOOKS

ISBN-13: 978-0-373-67466-4

OUT OF TIME

Copyright © 2011 by Harlequin Books S.A.

All rights reserved. Except for use in any review, the reproduction or utilization of this work in whole or in part in any form by any electronic, mechanical or other means, now known or hereafter invented, including xerography, photocopying and recording, or in any information storage or retrieval system, is forbidden without the written permission of the editorial office, Love Inspired Books, 233 Broadway, New York, NY 10279 U.S.A.

This is a work of fiction. Names, characters, places and incidents are either the product of the author's imagination or are used fictitiously, and any resemblance to actual persons, living or dead, business establishments, events or locales is entirely coincidental.

This edition published by arrangement with Love Inspired Books,

® and TM are trademarks of Love Inspired Books, used under license. Trademarks indicated with ® are registered in the United States Patent and Trademark Office, the Canadian Trade Marks Office and in other countries.

www.LoveInspiredBooks.com

Printed in U.S.A.

Therefore do not go on passing judgment before the time, but wait until the Lord comes who will both bring to light the things hidden in the darkness and disclose the motives of men's hearts; and then each man's praise will come to him from God.

—1 *Corinthians* 4:5

Sarah Rodgers. Keep working toward your goal,
and eventually you'll reach it!

ONE

Silence told its own story, and Alamo Ranger Susannah Jorgenson listened as she hurried across the bridge that led to the chapel. Darkness had fallen hours ago and the air held a hint of rain. The shadows seemed deeper than usual, the darkness just a little blacker. Or maybe it was simply her imagination that made the Alamo complex seem so forbidding.

Imagination and too many sleepless nights.

Six months since Aaron Simons had attacked her, five months since he was killed in a police standoff just outside of San Antonio, and Susannah was still jumping at shadows. People were starting to notice. Her fellow park rangers were beginning to talk. Her life, the one she'd planned so carefully, the one she'd wanted ever since she was a kid, was slowly unraveling, and she felt helpless to stop it.

She shivered. Not from the cold. Not from the chilly breeze. From the darkness, the silence, the endless echo of her fear as she made her final rounds. She'd never known terror before Aaron. Now, it was her closest friend. Not something she was proud of, but something she acknowledged as she jogged to the chapel and flashed the beam of her light along the corners of the building.

Nothing.

No movement, no sounds, no reason to think she wasn't alone, but she couldn't shake the feeling that she was being watched. That somewhere beyond the beam of her light, danger waited.

Her cell phone rang as she walked into the building, and she jumped, her heart pounding, her pulse racing. Everything out of proportion to the moment. That seemed to be the story of her life lately.

"Hello?" Her voice bounced off the stone walls of the chapel, and something skittered in a dark corner to her right. She turned, her flashlight revealing nothing but tile floor and emptiness.

"Susannah? It's Chad Morran."

"What's up?"

"Just got a call from Captain Ben Fritz with the Texas Rangers."

"Let me guess. He wanted to know about our security plans for the 175th anniversary of the Battle of the Alamo celebration." A soft sound carried through the cavernous room. Rustling papers? Fabric brushing against stone? Susannah cocked her head, listening, but heard nothing but her rapid heartbeat.

"Partially. He also wanted to let me know he's sending a man out to the compound. They want to do a security sweep. See where our areas of weakness are."

"They're assuming we have them."

"Aside from Fort Knox, I doubt there's a place that doesn't. With the 175th anniversary of the Battle of the Alamo coming up, we can't afford to be too careful. The opening ceremony has to go off without a hitch."

"I know." There were more than a few high-level politicians scheduled to speak at a ceremony that would be hosted by the Alamo Planning Committee, and protecting them was the first priority of the Alamo Rangers.

"So you won't mind staying at the compound a little late tonight? You *are* head of the security team for the event, after all."

"You don't need to convince me, Chad. I'm happy to do it." Though staying alone at the compound after dark had become one of her least favorite things to do.

"Good. Good. Captain Fritz said his man should be there within the hour. I can come and help with the briefing if you want me to, or we can touch base tomorrow before we open."

"No need for you to come. I'll handle things."

"You're sure?" That he would ask made Susannah's cheeks heat.

"It's my job, Chad. If I can't do it, I shouldn't be working here." Something she'd reminded herself of one too many times during the past few months.

"I wasn't implying that you couldn't handle it, Susannah. Just giving you an opportunity to ask for backup if you need it. This event is a big deal. We can't afford to have anything go wrong."

"Nothing will."

She hoped.

She prayed.

But things went wrong all the time.

Good days turned bad in a blink of an eye.

"All right. I'll leave it in your hands, then, and I'll want a full report tomorrow."

"No problem." She slid the phone back in her pocket, did a full sweep of the chapel and of the office area beyond. Nothing, of course. There was never anything. She should be relieved, but all she felt was disgust at herself and her fear.

She ran a hand over her hair and tapped her Stetson against her thigh. What she needed was a little fresh air. A few minutes outside of the compound listening to the sound of people and the action drifting up from the River Walk and she'd feel more like herself.

"Sure you will," she muttered as she opened the chapel door and stepped straight into a broad, muscular chest.

Someone grabbed her upper arms, holding her in place when she would have fallen.

And she was back in time, hands wrapped around her throat, cutting off air, fetid breath washing over her face. Alcohol and evil and every nightmare come to life.

She gagged, shoving forward into her attacker, pushing her weight into a solid wall of strength as she tried to unbalance him.

"Hey. Calm down. I was just trying to keep you from falling." The soothing tone washed over her, the words rumbling near her ear as the man released his hold and stepped back.

Broad-shouldered.

A wide-brimmed cowboy hat hiding his eyes.

Not Aaron.

Of course, not Aaron.

"Sorry about that. I wasn't expecting anyone to be standing near the door. We're closed for the day, but we'll be open again at seven tomorrow morning." She cleared her throat, wiped a sweaty palm against her khaki slacks.

"No need to apologize. I should have knocked as soon as I got here. I'm Ranger Levi McDonall. My captain said he was going to call and let you know I was on the way."

"Levi McDonall?" Her childhood hero? Her best guy friend? Her first teenage crush?

No way could they be the same.

"That's right. You *were* told that I'd be coming, weren't you?"

"Just a few minutes ago. Come on in." She hurried into the chapel, trying to pull herself together. This was the Texas Ranger she'd be working with for the next nine days, and she couldn't afford to look like she didn't have things under control.

Didn't have *herself* under control.

She flipped on a light, turned to face McDonall.

He'd pulled off his hat, and his strong, handsome face was exactly the one she hadn't believed it could be.

Levi McDonall.

Her Levi McDonall.

At least, that's how she'd once thought of him.

He met her gaze, his eyes a richer brown than she'd remembered, his lashes long and thick. He'd changed. Filled out. Gone from brash teenager to confident man.

"Susannah Jorgenson?" He took a step toward her, his eyes reflecting her surprise, his full lips curving into a smile.

"That's right."

"Of course it is. I'd know you anywhere."

"I guess so. I spent the better part of nine years annoying you."

"Annoying? I wouldn't exactly say that." He smiled again, flashing dimples that would have melted the hardest of hearts.

"I'm sure you would if you weren't afraid of sounding rude."

"When have you ever known me to be afraid of that?"

"I haven't *known* you for years. As a matter of fact, the last time I saw you, you were a teenager with big dreams."

"And the last time I saw *you,* you had pigtails and braces." He grinned, moving farther into the room, light reflecting off his black hair and simmering in his eyes.

"I never had braces," she responded, not resisting as he pulled her into a bear hug, bracing for what she knew she would feel. Trapped. Panicked.

But the feelings didn't come, and she let herself relax into his embrace, let his warmth seep into her and chase away the chill that had dogged her for the better part of the evening.

"That's better." He stepped back, looked down into her face, his gaze touching her hair, her cheeks, her lips before returning to her eyes.

"What?"

"You were wound up tighter than a caged tiger."

"Not really. I was just—" Afraid of nothing? Jumping at shadows? She couldn't say any of those things. "It's been a long day. I'm ready for it to be over."

"I'll make this as quick as possible, but I can't

promise that we won't be here awhile. The Alamo Planning Committee is anxious for security measures to be worked up and in place for the upcoming ceremony. My captain asked me to come by and do a security sweep, check to see if there are any weaknesses that we'll need to address during the event."

"I'll give you a tour. Let you get a feel for the compound. Then, we can go over things in detail." She followed his lead, focusing on the task at hand. Secure the compound for the ceremony. Get through the next nine days. She could make a decision about her future as an Alamo Ranger after that.

"You have some security plans in place already, right?"

"Of course. We've been working on them since we were told the opening ceremony would be held at the Alamo." She led him into the office, gestured for him to take a seat while she pulled a file from her desk. "We can take a look at the plans before we do the tour if you'd like."

"Better to see the place first, I think. I moved back to San Antonio a couple of years ago, but I haven't been to the Alamo since I was a kid. Walking around the compound will familiarize me with it again. That will make visualizing security measures a little easier."

"Let's get started, then." She led him through the

chapel and into the compound. Shadows still edged the path, but they seemed less sinister, the silence less ominous.

She wasn't sure she liked what that said about her.

She'd been an Alamo Ranger for four years, and she'd never been afraid to walk the compound alone at night. That she was ate at her, turned her inside out, made her wonder if being a security officer really was what she should be doing. Made her question everything she believed about herself, her goals, her passions.

"You've changed, Susannah." Levi broke into her thoughts, and she met his eyes, saw that he was studying her with an intensity that made her shiver.

"We've both changed."

"We've both matured, sure, but there's something else. Used to be you were bubbly and excitable. Talkative to the point of frustration. Now, you're subdued. Quiet."

"And you're reading a lot into five minutes of reconnecting." She offered a smile that she hoped looked more natural than it felt.

"Maybe, but—"

"It doesn't really matter, does it? We're both here to do a job. How we've changed, why we've changed, *if* we've changed, none of those things are important." She cut him off, not wanting speculation to lead to a discussion she didn't want to have. Not with Levi. Not with anyone.

"Then we'll call my observation a point of interest and move on. How big is the compound?"

"A little over four acres. The ceremony will take place in the gardens. We'll have a stage set up there."

"And you have enough people on your security team to keep the area protected?"

"Yes. We—" A loud bang shattered the quiet, the discordant sound so completely unexpected Susannah didn't have time to think, didn't have time to panic. She ran, skirting the long barracks, Levi close on her heels. Another bang followed the first, and she changed course, racing toward the sound. A figure lurched out from behind the giant oak that had stood for centuries in the compound, and Susannah called out a warning, her hand on her gun, her body humming with adrenaline.

The intruder didn't heed the warning to freeze, didn't stop bulldozing toward her. Wobbling, but coming fast, knocking into Susannah before she could decide if deadly force was necessary.

She stumbled and went down hard, the pungent scent of alcohol and sweat swirling around her, threatening to drag her back to that night, back into terror.

And then he was gone, pulled up and away, slammed down onto the ground, Levi crouching over him, a gun pressed to his head. “Don’t move. Don’t even breathe. You okay, Susannah?”

“Fine.” She managed to get to her feet, managed to cross the small area that separated them. Managed to do it all without shattering into a million pieces.

But she wanted to shatter.

Wanted to fall into a heap of blubbering fear and let Levi handle the intruder.

“Susie. Suze. You tell him to let me go. You tell him he’s got no right to treat me like this.” The slurred words, the voice, they were familiar. The alcohol. The sweat. The stumbling, fumbling steps.

Mitch.

She should have known.

She hadn’t.

Fear had clouded her judgment, had almost made her pull a weapon she didn’t need.

The knowledge was a heavy weight as she crouched next to Mitch and signaled for Levi to let him go.

TWO

"You can let him up." Susannah's voice seeped through the haze of Levi's rage as he leaned over her attacker. The acrid scent of alcohol and sweat drifted up from the prone man, mixing with the softer, subtler scent of Susannah's perfume.

Susannah Jorgenson.

He still couldn't quite believe the stunningly beautiful Alamo Ranger he was going to be working with for the next nine days was the knobby-kneed tomboy who'd followed him around when he was a kid.

"He's trespassing on private property." And he'd knocked Susannah to the ground.

"Trespassing? You know I wouldn't do something like that, Susannah." The words were slurred, the man obviously drunk as a skunk.

"You *are* trespassing, Mitch. And you know it." Susannah nudged Levi's arm away, then helped the man turn over and sit up. Deep wrinkles and hollow cheeks told the story of too much excess.

Threadbare clothes and duct-taped shoes told the story of something else. Desperation. Helplessness.

Levi knew the feeling of both those things.

Had known them since the day five months ago when his former captain, Gregory Pike, had been shot and killed in his own home.

"I fell asleep. You know how that happens with me sometimes."

"You didn't fall asleep. You passed out, and I told you that the next time you passed out on the compound I was going to call the police and have them take you away and dry you out."

"Now, you wouldn't do that to me, would you, girl?" The man ambled to his feet, his movements slow and ungainly.

"I should. I really should." Susannah reached out and grabbed the guy's arm, holding him steady when it looked like he might tip over.

"Fell asleep is all. Woke up and thought I'd better get out of here before I got myself into trouble. Tripped and fell into the door. Knocked the lid off a trash can near the barracks. Sorry about that."

"Passing out, falling asleep, neither of them are things I want you doing here. Especially not after hours. Now, where were you? I checked this compound twice in the past couple of hours, and I didn't see you."

"Behind the barracks."

"You weren't there when we closed."

"Don't know about that, doll. I came right in the gate. Just like I always do."

"Which gate?" She took Mitch by the arm, leading him back toward the chapel.

"Houston Street. Came in near the museum. Couldn't get inside the building, though."

"Because we're closed."

"Then why's the gate open?" Mitch's words were barely intelligible, and Levi was surprised he was still on his feet.

"That's a good question." Susannah led Mitch through the chapel, ushered him to the doors, barely meeting Levi's eyes. He could sense her tension, see the frown line between her brows.

She'd said she'd locked up, checked to make sure no one was there. Now they were escorting a drunk off the premises. That didn't bode well for the overall security of the compound, but Levi wouldn't say that. He'd tour the area with Susannah, make a thorough assessment of its strengths and weaknesses and come up with a plan of action that would satisfy the Alamo Planning Committee and the members of Texas Rangers Company D.

"Do you want me to call you a cab? Have it take you to the mission for the night?" Susannah asked as she stepped outside the chapel with Mitch.

"I got a place to stay, doll. Don't you worry." The guy stumbled away. Susannah watched him go, the seconds stretching into a minute before she finally turned to face Levi.

"I need to go check that gate. You can stay in the chapel if you'd like. Look over the plans we've put together for March 6." She looked drawn, her face leached of color, fear seeming to hover just beneath the surface of her eyes.

Was she afraid of Mitch?

Of Levi?

Of the fact that there'd been a trespasser on the compound while she was in charge?

"We haven't finished the tour, so I guess I'll come along. I wanted to see the garden where the ceremony will take place. I also need a count of gates and entrance points."

"There are six gates plus the entrance to the chapel." Moonlight fell across her face, highlighting deep hollows beneath her cheeks. She was thinner than Levi remembered, her face leaner, her shoulders narrow. Not delicate, but not the tough tomboy who'd played street hockey with the neighborhood boys.

"We'll need a plan to make sure they're secure on the day of the event."

"Already taken care of. We'll have a Ranger assigned to each gate." She turned and led Levi back through the chapel and out into the compound, her silence so different from the Susannah he remembered that Levi couldn't wrap his mind around it.

What had happened to the excitable little girl? The adolescent who'd poured her heart out to Levi as they'd sat on her parents' porch swing?

She'd disappeared. Left a quiet, somber woman in her place.

A quiet, somber, *beautiful* woman in her place.

But, then, he'd always suspected that she'd grow into a beauty.

He didn't try to fill the silence, just kept his peace as they walked toward a long, low building.

"This is the long barracks. It houses our museum. The gate Mitch was talking about is just to the east of it. I locked it after we closed for the day, so there's no way it could be open. Mitch tends to drink too much, and then he gets confu…" Her voice trailed off as the gate came into view.

"It's open." Levi took the last few steps to the gate, scanning the street beyond. A few cars drove by and voices carried on the cold air.

"I closed the gate as soon as the last visitor left. Made sure it was locked." Susannah flashed a light on the lock and examined it.

"Has it been tampered with?"

"Not that I can see."

"Is it possible you forgot to lock it?"

"I've been doing this for four years, Levi. I didn't forget."

"You're sure?"

"Yes."

"Maybe another security officer—"

"We don't work that way. If another Ranger had been here, I'd have known it." She stepped through the gate, looking up and down the street as if she expected to see someone standing there with a key.

"If you locked it, someone unlocked it."

"Or the lock is faulty." She closed the gate, locked it and then tried to pull it open again. It held tight.

"Looks like that's not the case." He gave it another tug for good measure.

"I need to call my boss. Let him know what's going on."

"We should get a team to scour the compound. Make sure whoever opened the gate isn't still hanging around. Check to see if he left anything behind."

"Right." She pulled out her cell phone, speaking quietly as she hurried along the path that led to the chapel.

He followed more slowly, scanning the foliage and the deep shadows they created. It would be easy enough for someone to hide there. Easy at night, but easy during the day, too. He'd have security teams run sweeps of the grounds before and during the ceremony to make sure the compound was empty. Hopefully, it would be enough to keep their VIP guests safe.

He frowned, eyeing the fence that separated the Alamo from the rest of the world and the buildings that jutted up above the compound. Not good from a security standpoint.

He dialed Ben Fritz's number, knowing his friend and the new captain of Company D would be interested in the development.

"Fritz speaking."

"It's Levi. I just arrived at the Alamo."

"How do things look?"

"They'd look better if there hadn't been an intruder on the compound."

"What happened?"

"That's what I'm trying to figure out. Seems one of the gates was locked and someone unlocked it."

"Are there security cameras on-site?"

"I'll check into it."

"Sooner rather than later, Levi. We don't have much time to make sure the Alamo is secure."

"Trust me, I can hear the clock ticking."

"Good, because Hank Zarvy is breathing down my neck, asking for a detailed plan regarding the opening ceremony."

"He'll get it."

"When you're good and ready to give it? Because if that's the case—"

"You know I don't work that way, Ben. Especially not when it comes to this case. Hank Zarvy is an annoyance I'm willing to deal with if it means solving Greg's murder." He glanced at Susannah, saw that she'd finished talking to her boss and was watching him, not even pretending that she wasn't listening to the conversation.

That was fine. There was plenty she needed to know.

"The Lions of Texas are behind all of this. We know that. What we need to find out is what they have planned for March 6. If we don't, more people could die."

"We're going to stop them, Ben, and we're going to find out which one of them pulled the trigger on Greg. We need justice. For Greg and for Corinna."

"No one realizes that more than I do. There isn't a day that goes by that I don't tell Corinna that we'll find her father's killer." Ben and Corinna were as close as any couple Levi had ever known, their love for each other a palpable thing. They weren't the only ones who'd found love in the months since Greg died, and Levi was sure that if his old boss could look down from Heaven and see what had happened to the men and women of Company D, he'd smile.

"We'll get his killer. I won't rest until we do."

"None of us will. Keep me updated on what's going on at the Alamo."

"I will."

"And, prepare yourself. Zarvy wants to meet with you and the head of Alamo security. Breakfast tomorrow at his place. Eight o'clock."

"We don't have time for meetings or hand-holding."

"We don't have time to bury our heads in the sand and pretend the Lions of Texas aren't a widespread and growing drug-smuggling organization. Thanks to Gisella and Brock Martin, we've found one of their drug entry points on the border and thrown a handful of their low-level operatives in jail, but we have a long way to go before we bring them down."

"A long way to go and not much time to accomplish it."

"Does that mean you're going to be at the meeting tomorrow?"

"Do I have a choice?"

"Not really."

"Then I'll be there." He disconnected, met Susannah's eyes. "We're scheduled to meet with Hank Zarvy tomorrow morning. You know him?"

"He's part of the Alamo Planning Committee, so we've met once or twice."

"He wants a briefing on our security plans."

"No problem. Maybe *you* can brief *me* on what's going on while we wait for Chad to show up."

"Chad?"

"Morran. He's my boss. He's called in a few other Park Rangers to help search the compound. They'll be here shortly."

"We can start the search now. If someone is on the compound, I'd like to have a chat with him. Do you have an extra flashlight?"

"Sure, but searching the compound isn't going to distract me." She met his eyes, her emerald gaze wary and filled with questions.

"From?"

"Let's not play games, Levi. Something is going on. Something bigger than a 175th anniversary celebration and a few threatening notes."

"My office has been investigating an organization called the Lions of Texas. We believe they're behind the threats."

"The Lions of Texas. Never heard of them."

"Not many people have. They're secretive. No one knows who their top members are, but we do know they're working to open the Mexican border."

"Toward what goal?"

"They're heavily involved in drug trafficking. An open border will make that easier. My captain was investigating them before he was murdered. Now, we're finishing the job he started."

"Gregory Pike was your captain?"

"I guess you've heard of him?"

"I saw the story in the news a few months ago. I'm sorry for your loss."

"So am I." Greg had been a great man, a fantastic captain, a wonderful father. Now, he was gone, and there was nothing Levi wouldn't do to find his murderer.

"Come on. We'd better get started on our search." He pushed his sorrow aside, pushed his anger away, refused the guilt that always seemed to be just a memory away. If he'd been just a few minutes earlier, would Greg still be alive? It was a question he'd asked a dozen times a day in the weeks following the murder, but there was no answer. No way to go back and relive the moments after he'd received the text summoning him to Pike's house.

"Do you really think whoever came in would hang around and wait to be found?" Susannah pushed her Stetson down onto her head as they stepped into the compound again.

"I don't know what the motivation was for entering the Alamo after it closed, so I can't say if the person would hang around. Has this kind of thing happened before?"

She hesitated just long enough to make him wonder. "Six months ago, I was scheduled to open the compound. When I got here, the Houston gate was already unlocked. Someone had stolen the keys and used them to gain access to the compound after business hours. That time, we found out who was responsible."

"He's in jail?"

"He's dead. Killed during a police standoff a month later."

"Was he a Ranger here?"

"No."

"Then he knew a Ranger." How else would he have gotten the keys?

"He knew me." Her tone was stiff, her expression unreadable. Whatever she was thinking and feeling was hidden behind a mask of indifference.

Which meant it was a subject she cared deeply about.

Or felt deeply about.

"I'm sorry."

"Not as sorry as I was."

"He was a boyfriend?"

"He thought he was."

Her words sparked a memory. A news story that had broken a few weeks after Greg's death. A woman viciously attacked, clinging to life in the hospital. A suspect leading the police on a high-speed chase through downtown San Antonio. All of it ending with the suspect dead.

"He nearly killed you." It wasn't a question. He already knew that the girl he'd grown up looking out for had been brutalized and nearly killed. He already knew that she'd suffered things most people couldn't even imagine.

He knew, and he wanted to pull her into his arms, tell her everything would be okay.

"Let's try to stay focused on the present, okay?"

"Ignoring the past can't make it go away."

"Do you really think it's possible for me to ignore it?" She laughed, the sound hollow and empty.

"I think that you're a survivor. I think—"

"Don't." She raised her hand, stopping his words. "I've heard all those things a thousand times, and I really don't want to hear them again. I just want…"

"What?"

"To go on with my life."

"Susie? You out here?" A man called out, and Susannah turned back the way they'd come, eager, it seemed, to end the conversation.

"Near the gardens, Chad."

Seconds later, a tall, lean man in his fifties strode into view. He met Levi's eyes, offered a brief handshake. "Chad Morran. I'm chief of security here."

"Ranger Levi McDonall."

"Not a good night to be at the Alamo, I'm afraid. We usually don't have this kind of trouble."

"Better to have it now than on the day of the ceremony."

"True. You've already checked the area?" Chad ran a hand down his jaw, his gaze jumping to Susannah.

"Not the entire compound, but we're working toward it. So far, everything is clear."

"Good. How about we split up? We'll finish more quickly that way. Ranger McDonall, you want to head east? Susannah, you check the gardens. I'll check the west gates. When Marcus and Larry get here, they can join in the fun."

"I'm not sure I'd call this fun," Susannah muttered under her breath, but Levi heard. She clutched a flashlight, her knuckles white as she started toward the gardens. She had a confident, brisk stride and easy movements, but he sensed her fear, wondered if it followed her the way his guilt followed him. Clinging, clutching, refusing to be ignored. If so, it was a heavy burden to bear.

He thought about going after her, asking her more about what she'd been through, what she was still going through, but he'd come to the Alamo to do a job. He couldn't afford to be distracted.

But you already have been.

The thought followed him as he turned on his flashlight and walked across the compound.

THREE

Susannah had never been afraid of the dark. Not when she was a kid. Not when she was a teenager. Not even when she'd started her job at the Alamo and learned the shadows and silence of the compound at night. Now, twenty-eight years into her life and four years into her job, Susannah was terrified of the black corners of the garden, the dingy gray-yellow of the path.

And that made her angry.

Angry at herself.

Angry at Aaron for stealing her sense of security.

Even angry at God.

She'd spent her life believing she'd weather any storm with her faith intact, her relationship with God certain even in the face of difficulties.

And then Aaron had come along, and everything she'd believed had changed.

The beam of her light jumped across the ground as she moved through the small garden. She trained it on a line of shrubs, following the greenery to the end of the garden wall. Nothing there. No one lurking in the shadows.

Her radio sputtered to life, and she jumped, her heart pounding in her chest.

"Susannah, where are you?" Chad's gruff voice carried over the radio.

"Just finishing in the garden."

"Find anything?"

"No. Everything is in order."

"Everything is clear on my end, too. Marcus and Larry are here, so if you're done, you can head home. I want the entire team here at six tomorrow morning. We need to figure out how this happened and make sure it doesn't happen again."

"I'll be here, but I have a meeting with Hank Zarvy at eight. He wants a briefing on security measures for the opening ceremony."

"When did he set that up?"

"He called the Texas Rangers to make the request, so I'm not sure."

"Request? Not much is a request when it comes from Zarvy."

"Fortunately, I don't have to deal with him on a regular basis."

"Want me to come to the meeting with you?"

"That's not necessary. Levi will be there if I need backup." *Levi.* She said the name as if they were good friends rather than business associates. If Chad noticed he didn't comment.

"All right. You'll let me know how it goes, right?"

"Of course."

"Good. Now, go on home. You've been here long enough."

"I don't mind staying."

"I know you don't, but it's not necessary."

"All right. I'll check in with Ranger McDonall, and then I'll be on my way. See you tomorrow." She shoved the radio back into its place on her belt. She wanted to go home. She did. What she *didn't* want to do was walk out of the compound, navigate the half mile to the parking lot where she'd left her Mustang. San Antonio was safe enough, and the parking lot where she'd left her car was well lit, but she felt like a walking bull's-eye at night, a victim waiting to be preyed upon.

She frowned, hurrying into the chapel and grabbing her purse from a locked file cabinet in the office.

A victim?

No. She was a survivor, and she wouldn't let what she'd lived through change that. She would walk out of the Alamo, she would walk to her car, and she'd do it with ease. Just as she had before Aaron entered her life.

She shoved the folder with the security details back in her desk and opened the office door, ready to find Levi, say good-night and be on her way. Chad was right. She'd been there plenty long enough, and the thick silence and hushed stillness of the place was eating at her, making her imagine things that weren't there.

She stepped out of the office and straight into a warm, hard chest.

"Seems like we keep running into each other." Levi cupped her arms, the heat of his palms seeping through her jacket and racing along her nerves.

Her cheeks heated, but she didn't jump back, didn't try to move away. That would say too much about her state of mind, too much about how hard she had to try to keep from falling apart. "I was just coming to look for you."

"Yeah?" He slid his hands down her arms, his fingers lingering on her elbows for a moment before he let go and stepped back. Looked down into her face.

"Chad is sending me home. I wanted to say good-night and finalize our plans for tomorrow. Did you find anything out there?"

"Not even a jackrabbit jumping through the bushes."

"I guess finding a guy sitting on a bench holding a stolen key would have made things too easy."

"I wouldn't mind a little bit of easy right about now."

"It's been a hard couple of months for the Texas

Rangers," she said, more to keep the conversation away from her past and her problems than anything else.

"That's putting it lightly."

"I really am sorry about what happened to Captain Pike. I know your entire team must be desperate to find his killer."

"Desperate is also putting it lightly." He offered a brief smile as he opened the chapel door and ushered her out of the compound. The air was crisp and cold, the night alive with the sounds of San Antonio. Cars. People. Life going on as it always did on Friday night. She needed to go on, too. She knew it. Knew she needed to move away from the past, move into the future, but she felt cemented to *that* night, cemented to Aaron's grasping hands and fetid breath.

Cemented to fear, unease, panic.

"You have a witness, right?" She'd heard that on the news recently, had been following the story with interest just like most people in San Antonio. Violent crime wasn't common there, and a Texas Ranger being murdered in his home had left the community uneasy.

"He's been in the hospital since the night of the attack. He's still too weak to talk, but we're hopeful he'll be able to identify a suspect soon."

"So, in all these months, you've gotten nothing out of him?"

"I wouldn't say that. He's been gesturing to a picture of the Alamo that's on the wall of his hospital room. We believe he's trying to warn us about a planned attack on the compound. The timing makes sense. The Alamo Planning Committee commissioned several high-ranking politicians to speak, and it would be the perfect time for the Lions of Texas to make a move."

"A move toward what?"

"Political footing, maybe." He shrugged, and Susannah could almost feel his frustration, *could* feel the tension that rolled off him.

"You'll find your answers, Levi." She touched his arm just as she would have fourteen years ago, felt the same instant connection, the same certainty of herself and her place in the world that she'd felt when she'd been too young to realize that the childish love she'd had for Levi couldn't last.

That surprised her, and she let her hand drop away, rubbing her fingers against her jacket, trying to wipe away his warmth and her response to it.

"I have no doubt about that, Susie. What I'm worried about is finding answers *before* the opening ceremony."

"We have over a week. That's a good amount of time."

"It's nothing compared to the months we've already spent searching for answers, but numbering our days isn't going to help secure the Alamo. Do you have security cameras at the compound?"

"Yes. I'm sure Chad will take a look at the tapes tonight. We're going to meet at six in the morning to discuss what happened."

"Just you and Chad?"

"The entire park Ranger team."

"Good. I'd like to meet your people, and I'd like to take a look at the security footage. Someone opened that gate, and, if we're lucky, the tapes will show us who."

"I've never been real keen on luck," Susannah said, stopping at the head of the alley that led to the parking lot and her Mustang.

She needed to say goodbye.

Let Levi go on his way.

But the dark alley seemed to pulse with life, the shadows reeked of danger.

She hated this part of her day. The shifting from busyness to quiet left her with too much time to think and too many memories waiting to drag her down into terror.

"Just a turn of phrase, Susie. God provides the answers, He orchestrates the timing. I just wish He'd move a little more quickly on this."

"That's the most difficult thing about faith. Holding on to it even when things don't work out how we want or *when* we want. Waiting for answers to prayer? It's killer."

"What answers are you waiting for?"

"Healing. Peace," she answered honestly.

"They'll come." His knuckles skimmed down her cheek, the touch featherlight and barely there, but she felt it to the depth of her soul. That connection, that knowing. Her body responding to memories of better times and happier days.

"I need to go." She forced herself to move away.

"Where are you parked?"

"Just on the other side of the alley."

"I'll walk you to your car." He didn't give her a chance to protest, just took her arm and started walking.

Darkness pressed in as they moved deeper into the alley, and she shivered, her heart beating double-time. Could he feel her pounding pulse? Did he sense her terror?

Susannah tried to still her frantic breathing, hold her panic in, but it bubbled out in tremors that shook her body.

"It's okay." His words were as gentle as his touch had been, his voice washing over her and stealing away some of her fear.

"I know."

"Then why are you shaking?"

"Because I hate the dark. I hate what could be hiding in it."

"Nothing is here that we can't deal with together."

"You're wrong, Levi. What's inside of me? The

fear I feel every day? That's something I have to deal with alone."

"Not anymore."

"Do you think that because you've walked back into my life, all my problems will be solved?" She laughed, the sound as dry and used up as she felt.

"What I think is that two people together can do a whole lot more than one person alone."

"Then maybe we should concentrate on coming up with a plan for dealing with Hank Zarvy. That seems like a lot better use of our time than worrying about how to change what I feel."

"Worrying about you could never be a waste of my time."

"Levi, it's been fourteen years, and we've barely thought of each other in that time. I don't think you need to worry about me."

"Who said I've barely thought about you?"

"You didn't try to contact me. I didn't try to contact you. Once you left for college, we both went on with our lives. But, like I said, we have more important things to do than chat about the past or about my issues."

Issues?

That made it sound like she had a penchant for dating the wrong guy or a spending problem or maybe even a tiny problem with alcohol.

Issues were little things.

Aaron was huge. What he'd done, what he'd

stolen from her, had carved an empty spot in her soul, left her open and wounded and bleeding.

And desperate for the kind of healing she wasn't sure she'd ever find.

"Like *I* said, ignoring the past doesn't make it go away."

"We need to come up with a plan for tomorrow. I've dealt with Zarvy on a couple of occasions. He's not an easy personality."

"Not a very subtle change of subjects, Susie."

"I didn't mean for it to be."

"So, we'll do things your way. Zarvy can be easy-going when he wants to be."

"Generally, he doesn't want to be."

"True, but he wants to make sure the ceremony goes off without a hitch. I think he'll be eager to cooperate with whatever plans we put into place. We didn't get a chance to go over your security plans, but we can do that tomorrow. I'll meet you at the Alamo before the meeting. Say five-thirty? We can drive over to Zarvy's place together after Morran briefs your team."

"I'll take my car and follow you."

"That would be a waste of gas. Besides, we can finalize any details on the way to Zarvy's place."

"I—" He was right. Of course he was. Riding together was reasonable, and Susannah had been trying for months to do reasonable things. Get up. Go to work. Refuse to give in to the temptation to structure every moment of every day around her fear. “All right. That sounds good.”

“Is this where you’re parked?” He gestured to a small parking lot in front of an old brick building.

“Yes.” She’d parked beneath a streetlight in the middle of the lot, and she crossed the pavement quickly, Levi keeping pace beside her. Light spilled down onto the car, bathing it in a pale yellow glow, and Susannah’s blood ran cold as she caught sight of something lying on its hood. A single rose. Deep red or black. She reached out, stopping short of picking it up.

A single rose.

Like the ones Aaron had left on her front porch, on her desk at work, on her bed. She shuddered, taking an unconscious step back and bumping into Levi.

“Looks like someone left you a gift.” His hands cupped her arms, holding her steady, but she barely felt his touch. Couldn’t feel anything but the terror that was taking hold.

“Looks like it.” Her voice was as brittle and dry as old bones.

“Are you going to take it?”

“No.”

“I guess there’s a reason why not.” He didn’t ask, though, and she didn’t say. Didn’t dare try to say. If she did, she might shatter into a million pieces.

He lifted the rose and held it up to the light. It

was a perfect velvety blossom, the thorns removed from the stem.

Susannah swayed, her heart skipping one beat and then another, her breath coming so quick and fast she felt dizzy.

"Susannah?" Levi let the rose drop to the ground, and it lay there like a snake. She could almost imagine it coming to life, slithering close and striking.

"Take a deep breath, Susie. Now!" Levi pushed back his hat and leaned close, looking straight into her eyes, his gaze as compelling and demanding as his voice.

She couldn't refuse him, and she drew in a deep breath and then another, oxygen flooding her brain.

Just a rose.

That was all it was.

No need to panic. No need to get upset.

"I'm okay. I'm fine," she said more to herself than to Levi.

"You don't look fine."

"I just...don't like roses." She opened the car door, slid into the front seat, her muscles trembling as the panic eased.

"Maybe I should get my car and follow you home."

"It's a seven-mile drive to my place. I'll be fine." She shoved the key in the ignition, forcing herself to meet Levi's eyes, to smile past the sick churning fear in her stomach.

"I see a lot more than dislike in your face. What's really going on?"

She'd known he would ask, but she didn't want to answer. Didn't want to tell him more of her secrets. Didn't want to see the pity in his eyes again.

"I already told you."

"Susannah—"

"We both have to be up before dawn. Let's call it a day and say good-night. Here's my business card. If something comes up, and you can't make it to the meeting tomorrow, just give me a call."

His jaw tightened, but he took the card. "Nothing will come up. I'll see you in the morning."

"See you then." She offered another smile, this one less shaky than the last, and shut the door.

Levi was still standing under the streetlight as she pulled out of the parking lot, his hat tilted back, his arms crossed over his chest.

The rose lay on the ground beside him, a dark line on the pavement.

A rose without a thorn.

She shivered, turning her gaze away.

She hated roses.

Hated them.

But that didn't mean the rose was a harbinger of danger. Anyone could have left it there. A friend. A coworker. Someone who'd wanted to cheer her up.

Maybe it hadn't even been meant for her. Maybe some hapless suitor had left it on the wrong car.

Please, God, let that be the case.

Because Susannah didn't want to go back to those months of terror, those endless weeks spent feeling as if every move she made, every word she said was being watched. She didn't want to go back to the nightmare she'd lived.

She turned on the radio, cruising the stations until she found something upbeat and light. Anything to fill the silence and refocus her thoughts. Tomorrow would be another long day, and she needed to be ready for it.

Prayed she'd be ready for it.

She could not mess up this assignment. Could not let fear get the best of her.

The rose had been nothing.

The unlocked gate had been nothing.

Just flukes.

She had to believe that or she might climb into bed, pull the covers over her head and stay there.

FOUR

The alarm went off at four-thirty, and Susannah fumbled to turn it off. She needed to drag herself out of bed, get showered and dressed and ready for work, but all she really wanted to do was stay exactly where she was, locked in her bedroom, locked in her house, safe from the world.

She frowned, forcing herself up and out of the bedroom. There were days when she thought it would be too easy to give in and watch from the window as the world passed by. Plenty of days, but she knew what a slippery slope that would be. One day at home. Then another. Before she knew it, she'd never leave.

She showered quickly, trying not to look too closely at the scar that bisected her abdomen. It had faded to pale lavender, but it was still a stark reminder of how close she'd come to dying. There were other scars. A small one on her rib cage. A deep one on her palm. A dark purple crescent below the hollow of her throat.

She buttoned her uniform to the neck, hiding the darkest scar. She wasn't ashamed of it, but she'd been asked about it too many times, and she was tired of the shock and pity she saw in people's eyes when she answered. It would be even worse to see that shock and pity in Levi's eyes.

Not that he didn't already know what she'd been through.

She'd seen recognition in his eyes when she'd told him about Aaron's death. No doubt, he'd remembered the news story and knew why Aaron had been running from the police.

He hadn't asked for details.

At least there was that.

She pulled her hair into a ponytail, leaning close to the mirror and touching the dark shadows beneath her eyes. She looked as tired as she felt, her freckles contrasting too sharply with her pale skin. She brushed on some blush, dabbed gloss on dry lips and shoved her Stetson over her hair. Enough staring in the mirror. She had a meeting to attend, breakfast to get through, another day to navigate.

And Levi back in her life after fourteen years.

She wasn't sure how she felt about that.

She stepped outside, inhaling cold, clean air, trying to clear her mind, ready herself for the day. God had a plan. She knew it, had clung to that knowledge even during the most difficult times after the attack.

He had a plan.

He'd see it through.

That was good enough. It had to be.

She'd always loved early morning, loved the silence before dawn. What she didn't like was the darkness that hovered at the edges of her well-lit porch, the shadows that swayed and swooped across the yard.

All she had to do was step off the porch, walk a few feet to her car and drive to the Alamo. Such an easy thing. Something that millions of people did every morning. Something that Susannah had once done without thought. Those days were gone, though, and she listened to the quiet, searching the darkness for signs that someone was waiting to pounce.

She hurried to the Mustang, opening the door and sliding in, her heart beating too fast, adrenaline coursing through her. Her hand shook as she shoved the key in the ignition and started the engine.

Car headlights appeared on the street behind her, and she waited impatiently for the vehicle to pass. The sooner she got on the road and started her day, the better she'd feel. Keeping her mind busy and her thoughts focused was the only way to keep the fear at bay.

But the car didn't pass. It pulled into the driveway, blocking her from leaving. Cold with dread, she grabbed the cell phone from her purse as she stared into the rearview mirror.

Would someone get out of the car, or would it pull back out onto the street?

Should she wait to see or call for help?

She waited, her heart jumping as the door opened and a familiar figure got out.

Levi!

Surprised, relieved, she got out of the Mustang, walked to meet him.

"What are you doing here?"

"Looking for you."

"Well, you found me. Which is strange since I didn't give you my address."

"You gave me your business card. I typed your phone number into a search engine and got your address. I called and left a message on your answering machine about twenty minutes ago. Since I didn't hear from you, I thought I'd swing by and see if you wanted to ride into work together."

"Sorry. I didn't get your message."

"It's probably for the best."

"Why's that?"

"You would have told me you could drive yourself to the Alamo."

"Probably."

"But now that I'm here, you can't refuse the ride."

"Can't I?"

"Not if you don't want to miss out on the coffee I brought for you."

"Coffee?"

"Yes."

"With cream and sugar?"

"If you want."

"Then, I guess you're right. I can't refuse."

He chuckled and opened the door of a dark sedan, gesturing for her to slide inside. Warm leather, soft classical music, the scent of Levi's aftershave hanging in the air—they enveloped Susannah, filled her with a longing she hadn't expected. It was a heady reminder of what she'd once been.

"Did you sleep well, Suzy-Q?" He handed her a take-out coffee, his profile hard and handsome, his gaze focused straight ahead as he drove toward the Alamo. Dark hair peeked out from his broad-rimmed cowboy hat, and she knew it was silky and smooth, had touched it more than once when she was a kid.

"Suzy-Q?" The nickname made her smile.

"You used to hate it when I called you that." He returned the smile, the dimple peeking out of his cheek.

"I think I still do."

He laughed, the sound pouring out into the car, filling the empty spot in Susannah's heart that he'd left years ago.

And now he was back in her life, easing his way back into her heart.

But she wasn't the girl who'd cried for a week when he went to college. She wasn't the child who'd idolized him. She was an adult with too many problems and not enough solutions.

"You didn't answer my question." His words seeped into her thoughts, and she took a sip of coffee, trying to wash down the lump in her throat.

"About how I slept? About as good as could be expected. I kept thinking about that unlocked gate."

"You and me both. I'm anxious to hear what Chad discovered after we left."

"If he discovered anything. Maybe you were right. Maybe I did just leave the gate open."

"I don't think I ever said that's what happened."

"I'm sure you were thinking it."

"For about two seconds, but I know you. I know you're thorough in everything you do."

"You *knew* me."

"That, too."

"Levi…"

"What?"

"We need to keep this professional."

"Isn't that what we're doing?" He pulled into

a parking lot a few blocks from the Alamo and rounded the car as Susannah got out.

"It should be."

"But?"

"But..." The coffee. The ride. The way she felt when she looked into his eyes. It felt personal. Too personal.

"We're old friends, reconnecting after years apart. That doesn't mean we can't be professionals doing our jobs, too." He smiled, and Susannah wished she were as comfortable as he seemed.

"There's a lot at stake, and we can't afford to be distracted."

"I think you know that neither of us could be distracted enough to let our work slide. What are you really afraid of, Susannah?"

"Who said I'm afraid?"

"You may not have said the words, but I see it in your eyes every time I look at you."

The words were a splash of ice water in the face—the knowledge that he could read her so easily, emphasizing how personal things with him could become.

"I just want to make sure we understand each other."

"That would be a lot easier if you'd tell me what you're really thinking."

"I'm thinking that I don't need any more complications in my life. I'm thinking that is exactly what you are."

"A complication? I think I'm flattered."

"Don't be. The past year had been tough. All I want is to get my life back to what it used to be."

"That may not be possible."

"Why do you stay that?" She glanced his way, saw that he was staring straight ahead.

"Certain things in our lives happen, and they change us forever."

It was true.

She knew it.

But that didn't mean she wanted to admit it. Not to him. Maybe even not to herself.

"Like I said, I want to keep things professional between us."

"You're changing the subject."

"Maybe I am." She took out her key, hurrying the last few steps to the Alamo.

To his credit, Levi didn't press for more. Just followed her into the chapel, his silence weighted and heavy.

"We'd better get to work. The rest of the Alamo Rangers will be here soon, and I'd like to finish before they arrive." She spoke into the tension, hoping to ease it as she walked into the office and opened a file cabinet.

She could feel the weight of Levi's stare as she

spread a map out on the desk, but she didn't turn to meet his gaze.

He'd been right when he'd said she was afraid. Of him. Of what she felt when she was with him.

Because she really *didn't* need complications in her life, and she really didn't *want* them.

But Levi—he was different.

An old friend.

And when she was with him, she felt safe.

She scowled, jabbing at the map. "Each of the Alamo gates is marked. As I told you last night, we plan to have an Alamo Ranger stationed at each one. The garden area is to the west of the chapel. Our guests will walk in at the chapel, follow the path around to the gardens and be seated by paid ushers."

"They're vetted?" He moved close, apparently willing to switch gears.

"The ushers? Of course. The Alamo Planning Committee hired them, and we did background checks on all of them."

"I'd like a list of names."

"It's in the folder. All our preparations are documented." She handed him the folder she'd put together. Professional, together, ready to do the job. That's the impression she wanted to give, and she relaxed as Levi glanced through the information.

"This looks great. Will there be caterers on-site? Drinks served?"

"No. As I'm sure you know, there's a luncheon planned at the River Walk Hotel as soon as the ceremony ends. I was told your people were responsible for escorting and protecting our guests once they leave the compound."

"We have a team set up."

"Some of the VIPs have their own security, too." The vice president would come with secret service agents and leave with them. The governor would do the same.

"My office is working closely with theirs to make sure all the security details are in place. Coming, going and everything in between." He frowned, circling the long barracks with his finger. "You've got a lot of places for people and things to hide. We'll be bringing in dogs to sniff for explosives the morning of, but we'll want to be even more cautious than usual during the days preceding the event." He was all business, and Susannah was relieved, glad to immerse herself in plans.

"We can have more security officers on-site during that time."

"Your boss will approve?"

"He's given me free rein to make decisions for the team. I'll run it by him after the meeting, but I'm sure there won't be a problem."

"He must have a lot of faith in you."

"I have more seniority than most of our security crew."

"How long have you been here?"

"Four years."

"And the person with least tenure?"

"Six months." Marcus Portman had been brought in part-time while Susannah recovered from her injuries. His work ethic and willingness to take any shift had helped him move from part-time to full-time within a month of being hired.

"And he's fully vetted?"

"Of course."

"Anyone on the team you don't trust? Anyone with money problems? Gambling troubles? Drug use?"

"I trust all my coworkers, but I can't say I know them all well. We have yearly reviews and criminal background checks every two years."

"And you gave me a list of all the Alamo Rangers who will be working March 6, right?" His brow furrowed as he rifled through the folder.

"It's here." Susannah pulled out the last sheet, holding it out to Levi, her eyes widening as he snagged her hand instead of the paper. He turned it over, traced the scar with his finger.

"That was quite a cut."

"It was." She tugged her hand away, resisting the urge to hide it behind her back.

"A defensive wound?" he asked, but he didn't need to. Susannah was sure he'd seen dozens of wounds just like it.

"Yes."

"Are you going to make me keep asking questions until I come up with one you're willing to answer, or are you going to go ahead and tell me what I want to know?"

"What do you want to know, Levi? How many times I was stabbed? How many times Aaron choked me into unconsciousness? How I managed to survive after he sliced open my stomach?" The words spilled out, her frustration spilling out with it. Not frustration with Levi. Frustration with herself, with her scars, with the sick feeling of dread that came every time she talked about that night.

"It's a good thing he's dead, because if he wasn't, I'd kill him." The rage in Levi's voice took her by surprise, the heat blazing from his eyes, cooling her temper.

"He was sick. I don't think he even knew what he was doing."

"No amount of sickness can excuse this." Levi grabbed her hand, touched the scar again, his finger so gentle, tears welled up in her eyes.

She blinked them away.

"You're right, but we're not here to talk about my scars or about Aaron. How about we keep that in mind?" She tugged away, thrust the paper into his hands and poured another sugar into her coffee.

She had no intention of drinking it.

She felt too sick, her stomach churning, her mind filled with a thousand memories she'd rather forget.

She'd always prided herself on her ability to read people, to know criminals from upstanding citizens. But she hadn't known with Aaron. Hadn't even suspected until he started calling her twice a day, driving by her house for no reason at all, making himself too much a part of her life. By that time, it was too late.

She shivered, cupping her hands around the coffee cup.

"I'm sorry. I shouldn't keep pushing." Levi took the cup and placed it on the desk, then lifted her scarred hand to his lips, pressing a tender kiss to the ridged flesh.

She shivered again. For different reasons. For reasons she wasn't even sure she dared acknowledge.

"I guess being curious just goes with your job." She tried to laugh, but it fell flat.

"That isn't why I'm asking questions, Susannah."

"Then why are you?"

"Because I care. Because thinking of you hurt tears me up inside. Because I'd give anything to go back and change what happened to you."

"You can't. I can't. It happened. I'm living with it, and that's a whole lot better than the alternative.

So please, let's just get back to work." She pressed her hand to her stomach, taking a step away.

He didn't respond, just studied her silently, his eyes still blazing with fury and with something else. Something her heart responded to, leaping in acknowledgement and doing the kind of happy dance it hadn't done in years.

"Susannah? You here?" Chad called out from the chapel, and she did what any self-preserving, scared-of-the-dark, twenty-eight-year-old would do when facing down a man like Levi.

She ran.

FIVE

Levi let Susannah go.

He needed to get control of his emotions before he faced the rest of the Alamo Ranger team. He knew it, and he took his time sliding the loose page back into the folder.

What do you want to know, Levi? How many times I was stabbed? How many times Aaron choked me into unconsciousness? How I managed to survive after he sliced open my stomach?

Susannah's words seemed to hang in the air, echoing through Levi's head.

How many times *had* she been stabbed? How many times *had* she been choked? How *had* she survived?

He wanted to know, and he didn't want to know.

Because knowing wouldn't change anything.

It would only make him wish more desperately that he could have been there to save her.

He clenched his fist to keep from slamming it into the wall, knowing that his rage did no good.

He'd felt the same sick helplessness after Gregory's death, had spent weeks trying to control the rage that drove him.

"Ranger McDonall, it's good to see you again." Chad walked into the office a few steps ahead of Susannah, his salt-and-pepper hair damp and slicked away from a broad forehead.

"You, too," he responded by rote as he met Susannah's eyes. Her cheeks had lost their color and wisps of dark hair had escaped her clips. She looked pale, but lovely, her emerald gaze clear and bright and filled with emotions Levi couldn't quite read.

A man in his mid-to-late twenties hurried into the office behind her. Wiry and tall, he had a stooped-shoulder gait that belied his youth.

"Marcus! I'm glad you could make it back this morning. How's the wife?" Chad patted him on the shoulder, and the younger man offered a sickly smile.

"Not good. The doctor said the baby is going to come early. We're just hoping he doesn't come *too* early."

"I'm sorry to hear that. I've been praying for all of you." Susannah touched Marcus's shoulder, her scarred hand resting there for a moment before she pulled it away, her gaze jumping to Levi.

What do you want to know, Levi? How many times I was stabbed?

He thought he could read the question in her

eyes, thought he could feel her reluctance to share more of her nightmare. He wanted to touch her hand again, tell her that the only thing he wanted to know was how he could help her heal.

He'd failed Gregory Pike, but he would *not* fail Susannah.

"Sounds like the rest of the crew is arriving. Let's move the meeting out into the chapel. There's more room there." Chad's comment pulled Levi back to the moment and the job.

He hadn't wanted to take the Alamo assignment. If he'd been given a choice, he would have passed it on to someone else. Now, as Susannah took a seat beside him, he couldn't help wondering if a divine plan was playing out; God bringing two friends together again just when they needed each other most. Friend helping friend. It had the ring of redemption to it.

"I know some of you have plans for later this morning, so let's go ahead and get started." Chad addressed the group, his face lined with fatigue. He gave a quick summary of the previous night's events, then went over protocol, reminding his team that closing the Alamo properly was the only way to keep it safe from vandals. "So, here's the question. Are any of you missing your key?"

There was a quick rush of "no's," followed by silence.

Were any of the Rangers lying?

"This is serious business, people. We need to know how that gate was opened."

"Is it possible Susannah left it unlocked?" An attractive brunette spoke up, her gaze shifting from Chad to Susannah and then to Levi. She smiled, the gesture easy and inviting.

A few years ago, Levi would have answered the invitation with a smile of his own, an offer of dinner, maybe even a few months of dating. He'd wanted different things then. A little fun. An exciting woman to spend time with. A few hours of forgetting the stresses of work.

"Of course I didn't." Susannah responded with confidence, and the brunette offered a patronizing smile.

"It would be easy enough to forget, Suz, and it's not like anything was taken or the compound was harmed. If you *did* forget, it's not a big deal."

"I *didn't* forget."

"No. You didn't." Chad cut in. "I watched the surveillance tape. It clearly shows you locking the gate. An hour later, someone else unlocks it from the street and walks onto the compound. A few minutes after that, Mitch shows up and walks in."

"Mitch?" Marcus spoke up, his brows furrowed.

"Homeless guy. Likes to hang out here when he drinks," the brunette offered.

"I don't think I've seen him around."

"Probably not. He likes to hang out when Susannah is here."

"Do you have the tape? I'd like to see it," Levi interrupted.

"I called the local police in to have a look at it, and they took it in as evidence."

"Did you get a visual of the perp?"

"Nothing definitive. The guy was average height and lean. He had a baseball cap covering his eyes and something else distorting his features. Looked like a nylon mask of some sort."

"I'd like the name of your contact at the San Antonio P.D. I'll need to look at the tape." Levi jotted down the name and phone number as Chad dictated them.

"I told the officer in charge that she should be expecting you to contact her, but I'm not sure you'll glean much from the tape."

"Maybe I won't, but it's at least something to go on. That's a lot more than we had last night." Levi smiled and stood, ready for the meeting to adjourn. It was closing in on seven, and he wanted to take a trip to the police department before he met with Zarvy.

Not that he was gung ho about meeting with the cattle baron. If he'd had his way, he'd have left all contact with the Alamo Planning Committee to Ben Fritz. As the new captain of Company D, Ben had a little more diplomacy in him than Levi.

"Give me a call if you discover anything new, will you?" Chad stood, too, and a murmur of conversation followed.

"Of course. You ready, Susannah?"

"As ready as I'll ever be." She offered a half smile and walked out of the compound. Levi followed, inhaling the pungent scent of the river and the aroma of freshly brewed coffee. It reminded him of the years he'd spent working in a bistro on the River Walk. He'd known even then that he wanted to be a Texas Ranger, and he'd never second-guessed his decision to leave San Antonio to pursue his degree, hadn't thought twice about it when he'd been assigned to Company D and moved back to San Antonio. He'd known those things were part of God's plan for his life. Lately, though, his career path seemed as empty as his apartment.

He frowned, not sure why he was thinking in that direction. He loved his job, loved his small apartment, but ever since Greg's murder, he'd felt the emptiness of his dreams and known that life was too finite to pour everything into a job.

"You're frowning." Susannah spoke quietly, and Levi met her gaze. She looked pensive, her shoulders and neck tense with anxiety.

"So are you."

"This whole thing is really bothering me. Someone has the key to the Alamo, someone who doesn't have authorization, and we have no idea who. I'll be the first to admit I'm worried." She took off her Stetson and smoothed an errant strand of hair.

"Worries don't do anything but cause wrinkles and indigestion. That's a direct quote from my Grandma Ida," he offered, and was pleased at Susannah's soft laugh.

"I remember Ida. She was quite the philosopher."

"She was also right. Worrying about this won't change it, Susannah. All we can do is keep searching for answers, keep following leads and pray that we find our perp before the opening ceremony."

"If this is about the opening ceremony, why come into the compound last night? Why give us a heads-up that someone has the key?"

"Good questions, and I don't have answers to them. Yet."

He put a hand on her lower back, steering her toward his car.

"We'd better find some answers quickly, because I have a feeling Hank Zarvy is going to be demanding a lot of them. There's no way he hasn't heard about what happened last night."

"Doesn't matter what he's heard or what he demands. He can't get blood from a turnip."

"Another Ida-ism?"

"Of course."

"Funny, I hadn't thought of her in years, but now

that you've brought her up, I remember her vividly. She used to sit on your front porch knitting sweaters and coaching our street-hockey games."

"You know what I remember?" He opened the car door, waiting while Susannah got in.

"What?" She looked up into his eyes.

"I remember that you were the best goalie on the hockey team. No one could get a puck past you."

"Yeah, and I still have the scars to prove it." She laughed and shook her head. "You guys were brutal."

"Would you rather we have let you off easy?" He got into the car, started the engine.

"I would have taken your heads off if you'd tried."

"You were quite a kid. One of the bravest, most determined people I knew."

"I guess I was." Her voice had gone quiet, the animation seeping out of it.

"You still are, Susannah."

"You don't know what I am."

"I know what I see. A woman who fought death and won. A survivor who won't let fear get the best of her."

She laughed, but this time there was no humor in the sound. "Like I said, you don't know what I am."

"Suz—"

"We're keeping things professional, remember? Treating each other like coworkers rather than friends."

"That's going to be difficult since we *are* friends."

"*Were* friends. Now, we're two people who knew each other a long time ago."

"Ouch," he said lightly, pulling out onto the road.

"I'm sorry. That didn't come out the way I meant it to."

"Then how did you mean it?"

"We have a job to do, Levi. Discussing the past won't get it done."

"We have a job to do, and we'll be spending a lot of time together because of that. It seems like the past is going to come up. Whether we want it to or not."

"Maybe you're right, but there are things I won't discuss. Things that are private and that I don't want you or anyone else digging into."

"I'm not planning on digging."

"You're asking an awful lot of questions for someone who isn't."

"Maybe you just feel that way because you have things you're trying to hide." He pulled into the police station and parked the car, turning to face Susannah. She looked pale in the early-morning light, her eyes deeply shadowed.

"I'm not hiding anything. I'm choosing not to discuss it."

"Why?"

"Because..." She shook her head, her lips tightening into a straight line. "I don't owe you an explanation. Even if I did, we don't have time for it. We need to watch the tape and get to our breakfast meeting. I don't think Zarvy will be happy if we're late."

"I'm not sure I care how Zarvy feels." But he got out of the car anyway, letting the subject of Susannah's secrets drop. That was the way she wanted it, and he respected her too much to insist on anything else.

It didn't take long to check into the San Antonio Police Department. It took a little more time to meet with Officer Sharon Stanford. Petite and energetic, she hurried them into a conference room, gesturing for Levi and Susannah to take seats as she pulled the security tape from a plastic evidence bag.

"Glad you came by this morning. I'll be out of the office for the next couple of days. Daughter is having a baby, and she wants me to fly to Houston to be there for the birth." She shoved the tape into place but didn't play the footage.

"Is this your first grandchild?" Susannah seemed willing to make small talk now that the talk had nothing to do with her.

"No. It'll be my fifth. Of course, I'm just as excited as the first time. This one is supposed to be a girl. The other four are boys." Officer Stanford pulled a small recorder out of a desk drawer and set it on the table. "Seeing as how I have you both here, I thought I'd go ahead and interview you. We've opened a case at the request of Chad Morran and the Alamo Planning Committee. I need to hear your version of how things went down last night. Mind if I record our conversation?"

"I don't. How about you, Susannah?"

"That's fine." Susannah tapped her fingers against the table, anxious, it seemed, to get on with things.

"Want some coffee or tea before we begin?"

"We have a breakfast appointment with a member of the Alamo Planning Committee in less than an hour, so we don't have a lot of time," Susannah responded, and Stanford nodded.

"I understand completely, and I'll have you out of here in no time. Unfortunately, I need to interview you separately. If one of you wants to follow me, the other can stay here and watch the surveillance tape."

"I'll come with you." Susannah stood and stretched, her right hand open, the scar bright purple and deeply ridged.

A defensive wound from an attack that had nearly killed her.

The rage he'd tamped down threatened to rise up again, but Levi couldn't allow it. He needed to focus on the tape, find out if any useful information could be gleaned from it.

Susannah and Officer Stanford left the room, and Levi scowled, pushing Play and watching as the previous night's events played out. The tape was grainy and dark, but Susannah was clearly recognizable as she approached the gate and locked it. He fast-forwarded through an hour of nothing, pausing the tape when a shadow appeared outside the gate. He leaned close to the small screen, wanting to take in as much detail as he could.

He was about to play more of the footage when his cell phone rang. He answered quickly, his gaze still on the screen.

"McDonall."

"Levi? It's Gisella." Texas Ranger Gisella Hernandez's voice carried across the line, and Levi straightened in his seat, turning away from the screen.

"It's a little early in the morning for a phone call, isn't it?"

"It's closing in on seven-thirty, Ranger, and we're both up and active, so why not?"

"You didn't know I'd be awake when you called." He stated the obvious, and she laughed.

"True, but I've been pacing this hospital room since four this morning. I need news. *Any* news." After being wounded in the line of duty, Gisella had been assigned to work at the hospital, guarding the only witness to Greg's murder, Quin Morton. Obviously, the gig wasn't nearly as exciting as she'd have liked.

"Wish I had some to give you. The Alamo is exactly what we expected. The security team is on the ball, but there are some holes we'll need to fill."

"I'd love to be there to help fill them," she muttered, and Levi grinned.

"Feeling antsy?"

"Feeling as if guarding our key witness is a waste of time. Brock keeps telling me to take it easy. Let things play out. He should know that isn't how I work," she grumbled, and Levi smiled. Gisella had found her perfect match in DEA agent Brock Martin. Together, they'd brought down several low-level members of the Lions of Texas, closed an area of the border being used as an entrance for the Lions' drug trade and struck a blow to its operations.

"Quin's still not talking?"

"Not unless you count repeatedly pointing to the picture of the Alamo as talking."

"He must be aware of how close we're getting to the ceremony." Levi hadn't been to the hospital in over a week. Being there was too frustrating. Morton had been critically wounded the day Gregory Pike was murdered, and there was no doubt that he knew exactly who the shooter was. Unfortunately, he'd been in a coma for months. Even after he'd regained consciousness, he'd been unable to talk and was too weak to write.

"Must be. He seems more agitated. He must have a lot he wants to say," Gisella responded.

"Then let's hope he's able to say it soon. What are his doctors saying? Are we any closer to him being able to speak?" Levi's gaze drifted back to the surveillance tape. Just a little more information. That's what they needed, but that seemed to be the story of their investigation into Gregory's murder. Every stone they turned revealed another stone waiting to be lifted.

"They're saying the same thing they always do. It's going to take time."

"Time we don't have if there really is something going down during the ceremony."

"We'll figure it out. We always do."

"Right," he responded, not wanting to point out the obvious—they didn't always figure things out. Company D had spent months searching for Greg's killer. During that time, they'd uncovered a drug ring and curtailed its activities. They'd identified a body and solved the mystery of restaurateur Axle Hudson's disappearance and murder.

What they hadn't done was find Pike's killer.

"You'll keep me posted on any new developments as we get closer to the ceremony, right?" Gisella asked.

"You know it. Take it easy."

"If I take it any easier, I'll die of boredom."

Levi chuckled and said a quick goodbye, pushing Play on the video monitor and watching as the gate swung open. A shadowy figure walked into the compound, keeping his face turned away from the camera. Someone who knew it was there, then. Someone who did not want to be recognized.

An Alamo Ranger?

Maybe.

The guy was tall and lean, dressed in dark pants and a thick jacket, a ball cap pulled low over his face. Chad had been right. It looked like the perp had nylon pulled over his face. His nose was mashed by it, his features blurred.

He turned his back to the camera, walking in what Levi thought was the direction of the chapel. He'd never shown up there. At least not as far as Levi knew.

Moments later, the guy was back, moving quickly, something in his hand. A stick? Levi paused the tape, using the computer to blow up the image.

Not a stick.

A rose. Long-stemmed.

Just like the one Susannah had found on her car.

Everything in Levi stilled, and he blew the photo up as much as he could. The image was distorted, but the rose was still clear.

A warning rather than a gift?

"What's that?" Susannah stepped back into the room, Officer Stanford just a few steps behind her.

"Looks like a rose. He didn't have it when he walked in, though. Can't believe I missed it. Guess since nothing was reported missing, I wasn't looking for him to be carrying something out." Officer Stanford frowned.

"He couldn't have taken it from the gardens. The roses haven't bloomed yet," Susannah said quietly, and Levi knew she was thinking about the rose on her car. The one they'd left lying on the pavement. He hadn't bothered picking it up. Maybe he should have.

"Is there anywhere else on the compound where he could have gotten one?"

"No."

"Then he had to have it with him when he walked in. Maybe under his jacket."

"Strange," Officer Stanford said, but Susannah didn't seem to hear.

"I need some fresh air." She pivoted, racing from the room before Levi could stop her.

"I'll come back for the interview another day."

He ran after her, Officer Stanford's protest echoing in his ears as he followed Susannah down the hall and out into the cool winter day.

SIX

Susannah didn't have keys, didn't have a car, didn't have anything but the fear that pounded through her, stole her breath, made her want to collapse in a heap on the ground. She wouldn't. Collapsing would be the ultimate humiliation, and she had no intention of embarrassing herself any more than she already had.

She'd seen the rose and she'd run.

Just the thought made her cringe.

She surveyed the parking lot, looking for a quick escape. There wasn't one, of course. It wasn't far to the bus stop. She could go there, catch a ride to the Alamo and walk home.

Then she could climb into bed, pull the covers over her head and pretend the day had yet to begin.

"Susannah!" Levi called, but she didn't want to answer. Didn't want to turn and face him after she'd bolted *because of a rose.*

Other people were afraid of spiders or snakes or dogs. Susannah was afraid of a flower.

She shuddered, stopping close to Levi's car and waiting as he jogged to her side.

"Hey, are you okay?" He touched her arm, the contact gentle as a spring breeze.

"Dandy." She blinked back tears that shouldn't have been but were, and frowned.

"Then why did you run?"

"Because roses give me the heebie-jeebies and seeing that guy carrying one out of the Alamo…"

"What?"

"Reminded me of the roses Aaron used to leave me."

His eyes darkened and he smoothed his palm over her hair as he had so many times when she'd been a quirky kid following him around from hockey game to hockey game, adventure to adventure.

She wanted to wrap her arms around his waist, cling to his strength until she found her own. But she'd never been that kind of person. She didn't want to *become* that kind of person—the kind who clung to others because she couldn't stand on her own.

She stepped back, forcing a smile she didn't feel. "Don't worry. I'm not going to shatter because of it."

"I know."

"And I'm not going to fall apart or collapse or—" He pressed a finger to her lips, sealing in the words.

"I know." His finger slipped away, tracing a line from her lips to her jaw to her neck until his hand rested on her nape. "You were always strong, Susannah. Aaron only succeeded in making you stronger."

He was wrong.

Aaron hadn't made her stronger. He had made her scared in a way she'd never been before.

"We need to get going if we're going to make it to Zarvy's ranch before eight. He's a stickler for punctuality." She stepped away from his touch, the heat of his palm lingering on the base of her neck as his hand fell away.

"You can't run from this forever." Levi stared into her eyes, his brow furrowed, his jaw set.

"I'm not running, I just don't want to talk about it. Not now."

"We have to."

"We will. *Eventually.*" She rounded the car, pulling open the door and getting into the passenger seat.

"*Eventually* isn't going to work, Susannah. That rose is part of everything else." Levi pulled onto East Houston, punching an address into his GPS as he waited at a red light.

"How can it be? Everything else is about the Lions of Texas and your captain's murder and protecting the Alamo. The rose…it's just a reminder of something that happened months ago."

"Tell me about Aaron." Levi's words drifted into the silence, undemanding and without emotion. He could have been asking her about the weather or what her favorite color was.

"I told you, I don't want to discuss him."

"Do you really think you have a choice? There are a half dozen high-level politicians coming to the Alamo next Sunday. All it would take is one explosive planted at just the right time and in just the right place, and we could lose our governor, lieutenant governor and the vice president of the United States."

"I know."

"Then you can't hold back. We have to figure out who the guy on that security footage is, and we need to begin with the roses and with Aaron."

"Aaron is dead. He's been dead for months. He has nothing to do with any of this."

"Then why the roses?"

"Aaron used to leave them for me. On my porch. On my desk at work. In my house and car. He even left one on my pillow once." She shuddered, remembering the feelings of violation and terror, the knowledge that her life was spinning out of control and that she had no way of stopping it.

"Who knows that Aaron was leaving them for you?"

"Anyone who knows me, I guess. I started getting them a month after I went to dinner with him. I didn't connect the two things at first. Later—"

"What?"

"He called me. Asked if I'd been getting the roses and if I liked them. Said he hoped they proved how serious he was about our relationship. I think that was the first time I realized that I was in trouble." And the first moment she'd really been afraid. There'd been something in his voice that had sent a chill up her spine and made her check the locks on the windows and doors. She still hadn't believed he would hurt her. Or maybe she simply hadn't wanted to believe it.

"So, you were getting roses, and that stopped after Aaron died."

"Right. I haven't touched a rose since...last summer." She stumbled over the words, not wanting to mention the attack, not wanting to discuss it.

"And then a rose appeared on your car."

"A rose without thorns. Just like the ones he left."

"There's only one reason someone would do that. He wants to intimidate you. He probably planned to leave it on your desk, but realized he wasn't alone on the compound and ran instead."

"Why would someone want to intimidate me?"

"Maybe he wants you out of the way before the opening ceremony next weekend."

"For what purpose? Even if I was scared enough to quit my job, there's still an entire security team to contend with. I'm just one small part of the security efforts."

"You're a liaison between the Alamo and Texas Rangers. You said yourself that your boss has complete faith in you, and that you're free to make decisions regarding the event. Maybe someone else would like to take your place. Maybe he's hoping to create a security plan that will benefit his cause. Who's in line for the position if you can't fill it?"

"I don't know. It's Chad's decision to make."

"So, there's no hierarchy?"

"No. He'd make his decision based on who he thought was best qualified to take over. I don't know who that would be."

"Could anyone else know?"

"I doubt it." She rubbed the bridge of her nose, willing herself to think. Someone had a key to the Alamo. That person had hidden a rose under his jacket and carried it into the compound. He'd meant to leave it for her to find. Levi was right. Susannah was certain of that.

"Can you make a list of everyone who knows about Aaron and also works at the Alamo?"

"That would be just about everyone who works there."

"That's fine. We'll be able to weed people down based on physical appearance. I'd also like to know who had access to your keys recently. Say, in the past two months."

"No one."

"You never left your keys unattended, didn't ask anyone to house-sit or water your plants?" Levi pulled onto a long driveway that led to a sprawling ranch. Golden-brown fields stretched out to either side, and cattle grazed as far as the eye could see. Green Bluff Ranch. Hank Zarvy's cattle operation. One that had made him a fortune.

"My keys haven't been out of my sight since I had the locks changed on all my doors. I even slept with them under my pillow when I was in the hospital. I knew Aaron was on the run from the police, and I was afraid he'd be waiting in my house when I was released. I'm still afraid that..."

"What?"

"I'm paranoid about my keys getting into the wrong hands. I worry that someone else will leave roses on my pillow or rifle through my things."

"I can understand that." He parked in front of the ranch, turned off the car.

"Can you? Because I'm having a hard time with it." She tried to laugh, but it fell flat.

"That's understandable, too. What happened to you—"

"Don't." She put a hand up, wanting to stop the words, refusing to hear his pity.

"It shouldn't have happened, Susannah. I'm sorry it did." Levi's expression was tight, his eyes glowed hot and bright. He reached for her hand, turned it over so he could see the scar, and she felt helpless to resist. Helpless to pull away.

He was so much of what she remembered—kind, charming, funny. But he was more, and she wanted to move closer, rest her head against his shoulder like she had when they were kids, let herself feel the easy rhythm of his breathing, the comforting thrum of his heart.

Surprised, she tugged her hand away, her cheeks hot. "We better get moving. It's eight."

Levi nodded, but he didn't move, just watched her silently, his gaze stripping away the facade she worked so hard to keep in place. Professional, successful, happy—they were the faces she put on for the world, but when she was alone, when she was on her knees before God in the darkest hours of the night, she was a coward, so scared of what the next moment would bring that she almost couldn't breathe.

She turned away, fumbling with the door handle.

"It's okay to be afraid, Susannah. Anyone who's lived through what you have would be." He spoke quietly, his tone gentle. That same gentleness was in his eyes when she met his gaze.

"It isn't okay, Levi. I'm a security guard. I'm supposed to have enough confidence to handle any situation that arises, but I have to make myself walk out of the house every morning. I'm terrified of walking to my car alone at night."

"There are plenty of other jobs—"

"I don't want another job. Do you remember my obsession with the Alamo when we were kids?"

"How could I forget? You used to insist that your brothers and I help defend a cardboard recreation of the chapel."

"I've wanted to be an Alamo Ranger since the first time my parents brought me to visit it. I won't let Aaron steal it away from me. He's already taken enough." The words slipped out, and she wanted to shove them back in, hide them in the deepest part of her heart.

"Sus—"

"We need to go." She opened the door, refusing to stop this time, refusing to do anything but walk to the ranch and the glowering bear of a man who stepped out onto the porch to greet them.

"You're late." Hank Zarvy didn't waste time with niceties, but Susannah hadn't expected him to. A hotshot in San Antonio, he'd made his money off cattle ranching and furthered his fortune buying and selling real estate. He had interests in many of the small businesses in town, and his charitable contributions to local homeless shelters and boys' and girls' clubs had garnered him the deep respect of the community. For the most part, he was an amiable guy, but Susannah had heard whispers about his temper and had seen it in play during a banquet he'd hosted at the Alamo when the short-staffed caterer served dinner late.

"We had a meeting at six and had to visit the San Antonio Police Department when it was over. We got here as soon as we could." Levi seemed unperturbed, his crisp white shirt and white broad-brimmed hat giving him a look of authority that most people would have acknowledged.

Zarvy wasn't most people.

He scowled, leaning his shoulder against the doorjamb and blocking their entrance to the house. "You could have called, Ranger. When you're on my time, it's what I expect."

"Good to know." Levi smiled, but the hardness in his eyes was unmistakable. "But I'm not on your time, I'm not on your payroll, and I have a job to do that involves a lot more than breakfast meetings."

Susannah braced herself for an explosion of rage, but Zarvy frowned, then nodded. "Sorry. I tend to get crabby when I haven't had my breakfast." He offered his hand, shaking Levi's with a vigor that might have taken a lesser man's arm off.

"No apology necessary. I just wanted to clarify who I work for and where my loyalties lie."

"Glad you did. I like a man who stands up for himself and stands up to me. I can be a little difficult to deal with. At least, that's what the wife says." He smiled, his broad face collapsing into a sea of sun-carved wrinkles as he turned his attention to Susannah.

"I know you, don't I?" It was more a statement than a question, but Susannah answered anyway.

"I work at the Alamo. I'm a Ranger there."

"I know you're a Ranger there, girl. You've got the uniform on. Don't you think I would have said it, if I'd thought that's where I'd seen you?"

"I stopped being a girl a decade ago, Mr. Zarvy, and I don't know you well enough to know what you'd say or what you wouldn't."

"Guess McDonall isn't the only one with steel in his spine. Seems like we grow 'em tough here in San Antonio. What's your name, Ranger?" He chuckled, offering Susannah a handshake that was just short of jarring.

"Susannah Jorgenson. I'm working as a liaison, helping coordinate Alamo security."

"Jorgenson?" He said it slowly, his gaze dropping from her face down to her scuffed cowboy boots, then back up to her face, and she willed him not to say what she saw in his eyes.

"You're the one who was in the news last summer. They didn't mention your name, but my wife works as a volunteer at the hospital, and she visited you during your recovery. Brought her silly little dog, Buddy."

Susannah vaguely remembered a woman bringing in a little white dog that had licked her face and made her smile.

"That crazy son of a gun tried to kill you, right? Attacked you in your own home. Nearly cut your guts out, but you managed to fight him off anyway."

"That's a slight exaggeration."

"It *was* you. Wait till my wife hears about this. She was talking about you for weeks. Come on in. Let me reintroduce you."

He walked into the house and motioned for them to follow. Susannah went quickly, feeling the weight of Levi's stare as she stepped into a large foyer.

A crystal chandelier hung from the ceiling, casting sparks of light as the sun streamed in through oversize windows. White marble tiles led deeper into the house.

"Edith! Come on out here. Wait'll you see who's come for breakfast."

"Mr. Zarvy." Susannah wanted to tell him that she wasn't a celebrity and that she'd prefer to keep her identity quiet, but Levi nudged her arm, shaking his head when she met his eyes.

He had a reason for asking her to keep quiet, but Susannah couldn't imagine what it was. She kept silent anyway, moving forward to greet Edith Zarvy as she entered the room, and wishing desperately that she were anywhere other than there.

SEVEN

Short and athletic-looking, platinum hair cut in a sleek bob, Edith Zarvy had an easy smile and sparkling eyes that belied her sedate approach.

"What is it, Hank? The way you're hollering, I thought the president might have stopped by for a visit." Her smile took the sting out of the words, her smooth skin and flawless complexion placing her at a few decades younger than her husband.

"Even better than the president. Bet you don't know who this is." He grabbed Susannah's arm, tugged her closer to his wife. Susannah's skin crawled where his fingers rested, and she shifted away.

"Susannah Jorgenson?" Edith looked surprised, and Susannah knew she remembered the hospital, the beeping machines, the weak and defeated woman who'd lain in bed and let her face be licked by a stranger's dog.

"Yes."

"You look wonderful! I can't believe it's really you." Edith pulled her into a hug. "How have you been?"

"I'm back at work, feeling good." Susannah shot a look in Levi's direction, hoping he'd read her unspoken words.

Get me out of here, now!

If he did, he ignored it, leaning his shoulder against a doorjamb and studying Zarvy through veiled eyes.

What was he thinking?

What did he hope to accomplish?

"I'm so glad. I've prayed for you often since the day I brought Buddy to visit you."

"Thank you, Mrs. Zarvy. Those prayers are truly appreciated."

"Call me Edith. Or Eddie. That's what my friends call me."

"Eddie is a man's name, and you most definitely are *not* a man." Hank threw an arm around Edith's waist and tugged her close to his side. She went willingly, but she seemed tense and somehow diminished, as if being so close to her husband had drained the life out of her.

"So you keep telling me." She offered a quick smile before turning her attention back to Susannah. "You work at the Alamo?"

"She's a Ranger, Edith. Can't you see the uniform?"

"I guess you're putting in extra hours, what with the 175th anniversary celebration looming." She ignored her husband, and Susannah shot Levi another look.

Another desperate plea.

Do something!

She did not want to be caught between a bickering married couple.

This time he seemed to get it.

"Sorry to interrupt the reunion, but we *are* busy planning for the celebration. If you'll excuse us, Mrs. Zarvy, we need to go ahead with our scheduled meeting." He offered a charming smile, and Edith nodded.

"Of course. I've got a breakfast spread out on the back patio. Please, enjoy yourselves." She hurried away, and Hank lumbered toward French doors.

"Hope you don't mind eating outside. I believe in a healthy dose of fresh air in the morning. Rodney Tanner, one of the other committee members, will be joining us shortly." He was all business now, his steps brisk as he led the way outside.

"Hank?" Edith appeared in the doorway, and he frowned.

"This is business, Edith. You know I don't like to be interrupted."

"I'm leaving for the doctor, and I wanted to say goodbye."

"Goodbye, then." His abrupt dismissal made Susannah cringe for his wife, but Edith didn't seem fazed.

"Susannah, it really has been great seeing you

again." Edith's gaze was so intense, so focused, the hair on the back of Susannah's neck stood on end.

"I feel the same."

"Do me a favor, will you?"

"What's that?"

"Watch your back." She shot a look at her husband, then disappeared again.

If Hank was perturbed by his wife's strange comment, he didn't show it. Just scooped food out of warming trays and onto an oversize plate. "Don't be shy. Come on and get some food. Coffee and juice are at the wet bar. You want something else, just go into the kitchen and dig through the fridge."

"This looks great," Levi said, motioning for Susannah to go ahead of him, and then dishing up a mountain of golden eggs and a pile of crispy hash browns.

Susannah knew she should be tempted by the colors and textures and variety of food, but all she felt was tired, Edith's words ringing in her ears.

Watch your back.

Why? Who did Edith think was coming up behind her?

She scooped up fresh fruit, dropped a slice of whole-wheat toast onto her plate and then joined Levi and Hank at a canopied table.

"You one of those women who's afraid to eat?" Zarvy frowned and gestured at her plate.

"I love to eat, but breakfast isn't something I

usually eat a lot of." That was the truth, though it wasn't the reason why she'd taken so little food. She felt raw, her emotions too close to the surface, and she wasn't sure she could swallow much more than a few bites.

"Glad to hear it. Seeing as how you're heading the Alamo security team, I thought I'd invite you to attend the luncheon at the River Walk Hotel after the ceremony. 'Course, I wouldn't want to do that if you're going to eat like a mouse." Zarvy shoveled eggs into his mouth, then took a sip of coffee, eyeing her over the rim of the mug. There was something calculating in his gaze, a sharpness that seemed in direct contrast to his jovial tone.

Before she could comment, he continued, turning his attention to Levi. "I'm sure your day is as busy as mine, so how about we get down to business?"

"Sounds good."

"You've walked through the Alamo?"

"I was at the site. I'll do a complete walk-through this afternoon, but the Alamo Rangers have been thorough in their plans for this event. I don't expect there to be any trouble."

"Good, because we want everything to go off as planned. Smooth, easy. No interruptions."

"We'll do everything we can to make sure that happens."

"Just make sure what you do is enough." Zarvy's

tone was sharp, but Levi didn't seem bothered by it.

"We're prepared, but things can happen. As I'm sure you know, even the best plans can be flawed."

"I don't want to hear about flaws, Ranger. I want to hear that the vice president and governor are going to get in and out of the Alamo alive."

"We've got no reason to think they won't."

"We've had threats. That's enough to keep me worrying until after the ceremony."

"The Alamo is secure and will be the day of the opening ceremony," Susannah cut in, hoping to move the conversation along. She had to be at work at noon, and it seemed as if Zarvy was talking in circles, reiterating the same points over and over again.

"Secure? You had a trespasser last night. Were you planning to tell me about that?"

"Nothing was taken or harmed, and we're still investigating." Levi's response was vague. Did he not want Zarvy to know about the surveillance tape and the rose, or was he keeping things close to the cuff until they knew more?

"Investigating? *Investigating!* The ceremony is in eight days. You don't have time for anything but resolution. Who was the trespasser? How did he get in? That's what I want to know. It's what you should already have discovered."

"Browbeating the help again, Zarvy?" A short thin man walked out onto the patio, his dark eyes flashing with humor.

"You finally made it. I thought I might have to send out a posse." Zarvy stood, shook the man's hand. "Rodney Tanner, this is Texas Ranger Levi McDonall and Alamo Ranger Susannah Jorgenson."

"I'm sure I've seen you both at committee meetings. Good to meet you again." Rodney grabbed a plate, scooped food onto it and sat at the table. "Did I miss anything?"

"I was just explaining to Mr. Zarvy that we're still investigating the incident that occurred at the Alamo last night."

"No leads?" Tanner seemed a lot more relaxed than his friend, and Susannah hoped that boded well for the rest of the meeting. She didn't want to spend the remainder of the morning defending Alamo security.

"Not enough to get a composite sketch of the perp. Hopefully, we'll have more to go on in the next twenty-four hours."

"Twenty-four hours? Didn't you hear what I said about—"

"Cool it, Hank. They're doing the best they can. Besides, we didn't call this meeting to criticize the work that's being done. We called it so that we could touch base, find out if there are any new developments. Your office was looking into those notes we received. Anything come of that?"

"We've done forensic testing, but there was no DNA. Nothing we can really sink our teeth into as far as following a lead." Levi finished eating and set his fork down. He seemed completely at ease, and Susannah envied that. She felt irritated, frustrated and ready to bolt.

"Too bad. The good news is, we haven't received any more threats. It seems like the person responsible has backed off."

"Is there some reason—" Susannah paused as her cell phone buzzed. She glanced at the caller ID, frowned.

"It's my supervisor. I need to take this. If you'll excuse me." She rose, walking several yards away as she answered.

"Hello?"

"Susannah? It's Chad. We have a problem." He sounded shaken, and that was so unlike Chad that Susannah's pulse jumped.

"What's going on?"

"Marcus found a box near the barracks when he was doing his rounds. It's unmarked and sealed. I've called the San Antonio Police Department, and they're sending the bomb squad to investigate. I need you and Levi back here as soon as possible."

"Bomb squad? Chad, are you sure—"

"I don't know, but we can't afford to take chances."

"We're at Hank Zarvy's place. It will take us twenty minutes to get back to the Alamo."

"Make sure he doesn't decide to come supervise the investigation. That man would micromanage a colony of ants, and that's the last thing I need to deal with right now. See you in a few." He disconnected, and Susannah turned, nearly walking into Levi. He cupped her biceps as she caught her balance, and she had the impression of harnessed power before he let her go and stepped back.

"Is everything okay?"

"Since you were eavesdropping, I'll assume you already know the answer to that."

"I heard the word *bomb.* I'm hoping it wasn't accurate."

"Marcus found a sealed package near the long barracks, and the bomb squad has been called in."

"We'd better get over there. Do you want to break the news to Zarvy or should I?" His palm rested on her lower back as he urged her toward the waiting men, and heat shot up her spine. Heat she had no business feeling. Not now. Probably not ever.

"I'll tell him."

He nodded, but his gaze drifted from her eyes to her lips, lingering there for a moment.

And she knew he'd felt it, too. That zing of electricity when he'd touched her back, the heat that was growing between them. Not the comforting touch of two friends reconnecting, but something deeper, stronger.

Her pulse jumped, her stomach flip-flopping as he raised his eyes, looked deep into hers. Levi the boy had been the fodder of many childish longings, but Levi the man wasn't just crush-worthy. He was much more dangerous than that, and she turned, nearly running back to Zarvy and Tanner.

"Looks like you're in a hurry, Ms. Jorgenson. Is everything okay?" Rodney Tanner's curious gaze pulled Susannah back to reality, back to her job.

"I'm sorry to cut the meeting short, but we need to return to the Alamo."

"Why?" Zarvy frowned, and Susannah braced herself for what she knew was going to come.

"Something was found on the grounds, and the police have been called in. They're bringing the bomb squad with them." There, she'd said it.

"What? Do you know what's going to happen when the bomb squad arrives there?" Zarvy shoved his plate away and stood.

"They're going to take a look at the box, and I'm hoping they're going to say there's nothing in it."

"Are you being flip with me, girl?" He spit the words out, his face nearly purple with rage. This was the man she'd seen at the Alamo. Demanding, unyielding and nearly out of control.

"As I said before, Mr. Zarvy, I'm not a girl."

"No, you're a little—"

"Cool it, Zarvy." Levi stepped between them, his muscles coiled, his voice tight.

"Cool it? We've had two incidents on the compound in less than twenty-four hours. What kind of security team allows that?"

"They don't have time for your temper tantrum, Hank, and neither do I, so how about you bring it down a notch and let the Ranger speak?" For the first time since he'd arrived, Rodney looked irritated, and Zarvy glared at his friend, then exhaled slowly.

"Right. I apologize. Seems like I'm doing that a lot this morning. Guess I'm on edge what with the celebration just around the corner. We've worked hard to organize the opening ceremony and all the events that will take place in the week following it. We're expecting record crowds. That's good for San Antonio's economy, and what's good for its economy is good for its people." He sounded so sincere, so truly concerned that Susannah's anger faded.

"I understand, Mr. Zarvy, and I want you to know that the Alamo Rangers are dedicated to securing the Alamo compound during the opening ceremony. Whatever has happened, it won't impact the success of that day."

"That's where you're wrong, Ms. Jorgenson. Once the press gets wind of things, it'll be all over the news, and maybe not just the local news. If some national news program decides to run the story, people will start to worry about their safety. Hotel and restaurant reservations will be canceled. The community will suffer." He shook his head, ran a hand down his jaw. "We're going to have to take care of this. Rodney, you call the *San Antonio Gazette*. Explain what's going on. See if George will agree not to run the story. I'll call the news stations, see if we can get their cooperation. You two go do your job. Make sure nothing goes wrong on the day of the ceremony." He issued the command and then walked into the house, disappearing down a hallway before any of them could respond.

"Well, I guess we've got our orders. I'll walk the two of you out." Rodney escorted them out the front door, offering a quick goodbye as he got into a Cadillac parked at the end of the driveway. The engine revved, and he sped away, the sudden silence following his departure almost deafening.

"That was fun," Susannah said more to herself than to Levi.

"A blast. Come on. We'd better get to the Alamo. I want to know what's in the package and where, exactly, it was found." He opened the car door.

"Chad said the barracks."

"That's close to the gate that was opened last night."

"Right."

"So, maybe our perp left it there."

"Then why not leave the rose?"

"Could be he planned to put that on your desk, realized the Alamo wasn't empty and ran. Or it could be that he didn't plant the box at all. Maybe it's a souvenir that someone left by mistake."

"It could be just about anything. Until we get there, we won't know."

"Let's hope a massive explosion doesn't clue us in before we arrive." Levi sped through downtown San Antonio and onto Alamo Street. A police barricade had been set up, and an officer checked IDs then waved them through.

"Looks like the bomb squad is already here." Levi pulled up behind the marked van, and Susannah hopped out of the car, hurrying over to a small group of Alamo Rangers standing across the street from the plaza. She didn't look to see if Levi was following. His presence was like a physical touch, pulling her toward him, making her want to turn around and meet his eyes.

"About time you showed up, Jorgenson. We finally get a little excitement and you're MIA." Shelley Radcliff grinned, her bright red hair peeking out from beneath her Stetson. Young and eager, she'd started working as an Alamo Ranger two years ago, but her real dream, she'd told Susannah, was to be a police officer.

"I'm not sure this kind of excitement is what we want around here. Where's Chad?"

"In with the bomb squad. The dogs already sniffed around in there. Looks like there aren't any explosives."

"Don't sound so disappointed, Radcliff. If there'd been explosives in the box, we might have all been blown to bits hours ago." Marcus stood a few feet away, watching a group of police officers move toward the Alamo.

"I heard you found the box." Levi stood beside Susannah, his hands in his pockets, his gaze resting on Marcus.

"Yeah. I was over at the barracks getting ready to open things up for the day. The box was in front of the door."

"Strange. I checked that area last night, and I didn't see it. I even checked the door to make sure it was locked. I need to go talk to Chad." Levi frowned and started walking toward the chapel.

"I'll go with you."

"No." Levi's sharp command nearly stopped her. Nearly.

"Sorry. It doesn't work that way." She fell into step beside him, ignoring his hard stare.

"What doesn't work which way?"

"Our partnership doesn't involve you issuing orders and me obeying them."

"This isn't a game, Susie. If there's a bomb on the Alamo compound, it could explode."

"There isn't. You heard Shelley. The dogs didn't find any explosives."

"I want you to wait here. When this is over, I'm going to take you home, and you're going to stay there until the opening ceremony is over."

She laughed at that. Really laughed.

"What's so funny?" He turned to face her, his eyes chocolate-brown and compelling. She could read his frustration there, read his concern, and she could see the boy he'd once been, the teenager he'd grown into. The man he'd become.

A handsome, compelling, heroic man.

And it would be so easy to depend on him if she let herself.

"I can't believe you'd really think that I'd go home and hide from whatever is going on here. I may spend half my time jumping at shadows, but I have a job to do, and I plan to do it."

"Even if that means putting yourself in the path of danger?"

"Isn't that what you do every day of your life?"

"That's different."

"No. It's the same. We're both professionals with jobs to do. Jobs that involve risks."

"I don't want you hurt, Susannah. That's the problem," he muttered, and then started walking again, leaving her with a choice. Follow him or stay?

It wasn't a difficult one to make.

No matter how hard her heart was pounding, no matter how afraid she was, *no matter what,* she had to be part of the investigation.

EIGHT

Susannah never gave up.

Levi had forgotten that. Forgotten how doggedly determined she was when she made a decision about something. He wanted to turn around and insist that she wait with the other Alamo Rangers, but she was head of the security team, and she had the right, even the responsibility, to be on-site with the other investigators. If she'd been anyone else, he would have been impressed by her determination.

But she wasn't.

She was little Susannah Jorgenson, the girl who'd stared out her window while he and his parents moved into their San Antonio home. She'd been five to his ten, with wild red curls and wide green eyes. When he'd waved, she'd smiled, and he was hooked, his ten-year-old heart smitten.

Maybe he still was, because the thought of her in danger made him want to scoop her up and carry her away.

"Susannah!" Chad called out as they approached the long barracks and a group of uniformed police officers gathered there. "I'm glad you're here. Take a look at this."

"What is it?"

"I'm hoping you can tell me." Chad said something to one of the officers, and he carried the box to them, his hands gloved.

"It's smaller than I imagined," Susannah murmured as she eyed the box.

It *was* small, maybe the size of a child's shoebox, and wrapped in brown paper that had been peeled back.

"The dogs indicated there were no explosives, and we scanned it for suspicious contents. There were none, but I can't say that this isn't a little strange." The man who held the box frowned, tilting it so that hundreds of rose petals were visible.

Susannah stepped back, her face leached of color. "Rose petals? That's it?"

"No. We also found this." The officer held up a photo that looked like it had been shot with an old-fashioned Polaroid. In the foreground, a bouquet of bloodred roses lay on lush grass. Just behind it a gravestone rose up, gray and plain, the carved letters clearly visible. At the bottom, written in bold black letters were the words—Your Fault.

"Aaron's grave."

"He was killed last summer, right?" the officer asked, and Susannah nodded.

"I'm afraid so."

"I remember the story. Not a good time in your life."

"It wasn't."

"But someone seems to want you to relive it. Is there anyone who might have a grudge against you? Someone who might blame you for Aaron's death?"

"No." She fisted her hands, relaxed them, fisted them again, the motion carving deep purple crescents into her palm.

Levi wanted to smooth his hand over the marks, run his thumb over her knuckles. Wanted to tell her that she didn't have to do what she was doing. Didn't have to look at the rose petals, the photo, the memories that must be screaming through her mind.

But he knew she did.

She needed to face her past as surely as he had to face his guilt. Come to terms with it. Begin to move on.

"Are you sure?" the officer pressed, and Susannah nodded.

"As sure as I can be."

"We'll do forensic testing on the box. See if we can gather any kind of evidence. In the meantime, if you think of anyone who might have done this, give me a call." The officer handed Susannah a business card, then carried the box away.

"This isn't good. We have one of the most prestigious groups of politicians we've ever hosted coming to the Alamo in a few days. We can't afford to have this kind of stuff going on." Chad raked a hand through his hair and scowled.

"I'm going to call my captain. See if he can send a man to look at the surveillance tape. Maybe we missed something." Levi took a few steps away and dialed Ben's number, his gaze on Susannah. She and Chad had their heads bent together and were talking quietly. She looked confident and at ease, but there was tension in her shoulders and fear in the depth of her eyes.

Rose petals in a box.

A photo of a grave.

The hint of a threat in two words—*Your Fault*.

It should have been an easy call. The roses had been left by someone who knew Aaron and blamed Susannah for his death. But Levi didn't think it was as simple as that.

Someone was trying to scare Susannah away from the Alamo, and he was sure that it had something to do with the Lions of Texas and their plans for the opening ceremony.

"Fritz speaking."

"It's Levi. There's more trouble at the Alamo."

"So Zarvy said."

"He doesn't waste time, does he?"

"Neither can we. Anderson is on his way to your location. We need to get this situation under control."

"Do me a favor and send him over to San Antonio P.D., instead. They have surveillance footage from last night. I'm hoping we can get a copy of the tape, have it run through our system. We need to identify the perpetrator if we're going to have any hope of stopping whatever The Lions are planning."

"Sounds good. You sure you don't need backup at the site?"

"Not yet." Levi explained the box and the rose petals and photo, mentioned Susannah and the trauma she'd been through.

She must have heard her name. She looked up, frowning.

"I remember hearing about that. The woman has been through a lot. It may be best to have her pulled from the Alamo until we get through the ceremony."

"I suggested she step down from her position as lead security officer."

"And?"

"She refused."

"Maybe the decision shouldn't be hers."

"I'm not going to make it mine."

"Your choice, but don't lose sight of your priorities. The Lions have already murdered Captain Pike and Axle Hudson. They're not going to hesitate to kill again."

"I couldn't forget that if I tried."

"Good. Report in if anything changes."

"Right." He slid the phone in his pocket as Susannah approached.

"Bad news?"

"No news."

"Which is just as bad."

"Right." He took off his hat, ran his hand over his hair, knowing what he had to say and what he wanted to say. "My captain wants you to step down from your position as lead security officer."

"It isn't his choice." She didn't seem fazed by his comment, didn't seem upset.

"No, but it might be a wise one."

"This is your case, Levi. I get that. You're after the Lions of Texas, Gregory Pike's killer. You're working hard to secure the Alamo and prevent whatever is being planned from coming to fruition. So, it's your gig, but it's my battle. All this." She waved toward the officer who was bagging up the box and petals and photo. "It's not just about keeping the Alamo secure. It's about me proving that I can still handle the job. Still do what I've always wanted to."

"You don't need to prove that to anyone, Susannah."

"I have to prove it to myself. I can't walk away

from this. I won't. Chad has gone to speak with the rest of the security team. We'll be running shifts for the rest of the week. Two Rangers here at all times."

"Susannah—"

"I know you could talk to Chad. You could tell him you want me off the assignment. I hope you won't."

"I should." But, he wouldn't. She had a right to fight her battle and face down her demons, and he had no right to take that from her. He just prayed he wouldn't regret the decision.

"I want you close to my side until this is over. When you're not here, you're with me or you're at home."

"That's—"

"Those are my conditions, Susannah."

"Fine. Home or here or with you." She frowned and stalked toward the barracks. Yellow crime scene tape cordoned off the area near the door.

"I guess that's where they found the box."

"Looks like it." She took a deep breath, and Levi imagined she was reining in her irritation, forcing herself to accept his plan.

"It seems to me that we would have seen it sitting there if it had been left last night. I walked by this area more than once."

"So did I." She frowned, surveying the barracks,

the grounds, the path they were on. Her gaze stopped on the gate, held there. "Do you think it's possible someone came in after we left last night?"

"Anything is possible. We need to check the surveillance tapes from every gate, see if our perp slipped in after we left last night."

"I was thinking the same."

"I'll ask Chad to take a look and then pass the tapes on to your office." She turned to face him, her skin satiny-smooth in the midmorning light. "There's something I need to say. Something you need to know before we start…spending more time together."

"What's that?"

"I don't want your pity. I don't ever want to look in your eyes and know that you feel sorry for me."

"Why would I?"

"Why does anyone? They see me as a victim. A woman who was brutalized by a man she trusted. Someone who might break at any moment."

"If I thought you were going to break, I wouldn't be standing here. I'd be having a talk with Chad. It's what I want to do, Susie, and if I didn't know how much I'd be taking from you by doing it, I would."

"I'm not a kid anymore. I don't need your protection."

"You're definitely not a kid anymore, but I remember when you were, and I'd never forgive myself if something happened to you."

"It wouldn't be your fault. Terrible things happen. Only God knows why. All we can do is hang on tight and trust that He'll see us through."

"Is that what you've been doing? Hanging on tight?"

"I'm hanging on by a thread, Levi. Barely making it from day to day, but I believe things will get better. I believe that God is still here, still with me. So, I just keep going." Her honesty surprised him, the tears in her eyes stealing his breath and settling deep in his gut.

"Don't cry. You'll break my heart if you do." He wrapped a hand around her waist, pulling her forward and into his arms. She felt strong and fragile, firm and yielding, and he wanted to soak her in just as he would the first sweet rays of summer sun.

"Like you broke mine when you went off to college and left me?"

"Did I?"

"Of course. You were *my* Levi, and I didn't think I'd ever have to let you go." She sniffed and pulled back, smiling gently as if the memory were as sweet as it was painful.

"Maybe you don't."

"I said you *were* my Levi. I'm not a kid with stars in her eyes and dreams in her heart anymore. Come on. We have a lot of work to do." She didn't give him a chance to respond, just turned and jogged toward the chapel and the group of Alamo Rangers that was converging there.

Levi followed more slowly, knowing he'd crossed a line that he wouldn't be able to step back over again.

Knowing, but not sure he cared.

His assignment at the Alamo would be over soon. Hopefully, they'd have Captain Pike's killer in custody and the Lions of Texas disbanded. He'd go back to his life and his work, but what he wouldn't do was walk away from Susannah.

He'd learned something the day Gregory was murdered. Life changed in an instant, so it should be lived without regret. Or maybe *learned* wasn't the right word. Being a law-enforcement officer had taught him everything he needed to know about how finite life was, how fragile, but he hadn't owned that truth until he'd seen his friend and mentor's lifeless body. Now, Levi lived what he knew, savoring the time he had while he had it, trying to live the life God had given him with integrity and honor. No rushing, no jumping the gun, simply waiting to see where God would bring him.

And where God had brought him was back into Susannah's life.

There was a reason for that, and Levi planned to stick around, wait it out and find out exactly where that would lead them.

NINE

The shrill ring of the phone pulled Susannah from restless sleep. She sat up, knocking the alarm clock off the bedside table as she grabbed the receiver and lifted it to her ear.

"Hello?"

"Susannah? It's Marcus Portman." He sounded frantic, and Susannah sat up straight, her thinking suddenly clear and sharp.

"What's wrong? Has there been another trespasser at the Alamo?" She shoved off her blankets, grabbed the clock. 5:00 a.m., and she could think of no other reason for his call but trouble.

"No. It's my wife, Deborah. The hospital just called. She's having contractions again, and they're worried."

"I'm so sorry." She'd met Deborah at a Christmas party at Chad's house and had liked the soft-spoken young woman. "Would you like me to put her on our prayer list at church?"

"If you want, but that's not why I'm calling."

He hesitated, and Susannah felt a twinge of impatience. Marcus was a nice enough guy, but he tended to skirt around issues rather than confront them. Whether it was a schedule he couldn't work or a problem with a coworker, he was much more likely to stew on it than to try to change it.

"Do you need help with something? Meals? Someone to stay with Deborah at the hospital?" She offered him a few options, hoping he'd choose one and let the conversation move on.

"I'm scheduled to work morning shift tomorrow. Three to eleven."

"You want me to take your shift?"

"Not the entire shift. I've already missed too many days of work, and Chad won't be happy if I don't show."

"I'm sure he'll understand."

"Maybe, but I can't afford to lose my job. I'll work my shift, but I was really hoping someone could fill in for me for the first couple of hours. That way I can stay at the hospital tonight and swing home before work to shower and change."

"How long are you talking? I'm scheduled to work night shift tomorrow. And I don't really want to work back-to-back shifts."

"I should be there by five."

"All right. Call me if you get held up."

"I will. And I owe you big for this, Susannah. Things have been really stressful lately. We've been trying for this baby for five years. If we lose him…" His voice broke, and Susannah's irritation faded away.

"You won't, Marcus."

"I hope not. *I'd* be devastated, but I worry that Deborah wouldn't survive. We've just wanted this for so long. Our medical debt is piling up. We're both so stressed we can barely think. Deb needs something good to happen. She needs this baby to survive."

"I really think he will. She's getting closer to her due date, and even if he's born now, he has a chance."

"The logical part of me knows that, but I'm still worried. Anyway, I appreciate you being willing to step in for me. I know you've had your own things to deal with lately."

"You mean what happened yesterday?"

"Yeah. It had to be rough seeing the rose petals and photo of that guy's grave after everything you went through last summer."

"I'm okay."

"You know, no one would think any worse of you if you took some time off. Let this big shindig go on without you. We have plenty of security guards working the event. Plus Texas Rangers."

"I appreciate your concern, Marcus. But I really am fine."

"I figured you would be. It was Chad who was

worrying. He said he didn't know if this would be too much for you. I said you'd handle it just fine."

"You were right." But the idea that her coworkers had been discussing her ability to perform the job didn't sit well.

"Anyway, thanks for being willing to fill in for me. I knew I could count on you." There was a cockiness to his voice that set Susannah's teeth on edge, and she wondered if Deborah really was in the hospital again or if Marcus simply didn't want to work the early shift. Irritated with him and with her doubts, she said goodbye and hung up, pacing across her room, pulling clothes from her closet.

It was early for church, but she could start getting ready. Maybe make some coffee and sit on the porch and drink it until the sun came up.

You're here, at home or with me.

She could almost hear Levi's voice, could almost feel his arm wrapped firmly around her waist, pulling her into a place that felt as much like home as any place she'd ever been.

She frowned, brushing loose curls from her cheeks and walking out into the kitchen. Coffee. She needed it. Something sweet would be good, too. And she'd stay in the house, tucked away and hidden from danger. Just like everyone seemed to want her to do.

And she wanted it, too.

But more than that, she wanted to feel confident,

brave, eager to walk outside and inhale the late-winter air no matter the dangers doing so might bring.

The phone rang again, and she stalked toward it. "Marcus, if you need me to fill in for your whole shift—"

"Does Marcus make a habit of calling you at five in the morning?" Levi's voice flowed smooth as melted chocolate, and she imagined him sitting in an apartment somewhere, his black hair mussed, his eyes still cloudy with sleep.

"Apparently, a lot of people are making a habit of calling me at five this morning. Is everything okay?"

"I just got a call from Anderson Michaels. He's a Ranger with Company D. He spent last night going over the surveillance tapes Chad sent him."

"Did he see anything?"

"Nothing. Of course, there's no camera aimed at the door of the barracks, so anyone who was at the compound could have easily left it there without being seen."

"The only people there were…" She didn't want to say it. Didn't want to believe it.

"Alamo Rangers."

"So, one of my coworkers is trying to get rid of me to make it easier to help ruin the opening ceremony. Is that what you think?"

"It's what I suspect, and if I'm right then one

of your coworkers is being paid by the Lions of Texas."

"I don't want to believe that."

"No one wants to believe someone they trust would betray them, but it's better to look at the facts than to rest on our emotions."

He was right. She knew it.

Hadn't she allowed herself to be swayed by emotion when it came to Aaron? She'd felt sorry for him. She'd wanted to believe he was harmless. He hadn't been, and she'd paid the price for her folly.

"So, we have a week to find out which of the people I'd trust with my life isn't trustworthy."

"We're running background checks on each of your coworkers. We're also pulling in a couple of Texas Rangers to help run security during the next week. Hopefully, that'll keep our guy in check until we can pin a name to him."

"Thanks for letting me know."

"Did you think that was all I called for?"

"Wasn't it?"

"I brought you something."

"Brought me some—"

The doorbell rang, the sound so unexpected, Susannah jumped.

"Are you going to open the door, Susie? Or leave me standing out here for another hour?"

"I *should* leave you out there for another hour.

This isn't the right time of day for visiting." But she went to the door anyway. Pulled it open anyway.

Because she'd never been able to resist Levi. Not when they were kids, and apparently not now.

"Good morning." He offered a smile that would have warmed the iciest heart and stepped inside, a white bag held out like a peace offering.

"I'm not sure how good it is when I'm standing here in flannel pajamas and bare feet while you smirk at me."

"I'm not smirking. I'm smiling appreciatively. I've never been much for flannel, but on you it looks good."

She snorted and took the bag he offered, a whiff of cinnamon and vanilla hitting her nose and making her stomach growl. "What is it? Sticky buns?"

"Better than that." He took the bag again, his fingers sliding against hers, warm and callused, strong and gentle. If he'd come back into her life before Aaron, she might have moved in close, asked for more than that brief contact.

"I remembered that these were your favorite when we were kids." He pulled out an oversize muffin, held it out to her.

And she swallowed back the sorrow she knew she shouldn't feel, swallowed down the lump in her throat. The tears for all the things Aaron had taken from her.

"Cinnamon chip?" Her voice was husky and tight with emotion, and Levi pressed a finger to her chin, urging her to look into his eyes. The compassion she saw there, the concern, only added to her sadness, and she turned away, walking into the kitchen, pulling plates and mugs from the cupboard. Starting a pot of coffee. Anything to keep from looking into his eyes again.

"What's wrong, Susie?" He set the bag on the counter, took the plates from her hand.

"Just…thinking."

"About?"

"How I used to dream that one day you'd bring me flowers and chocolates and treats." She tried to smile. Failed.

"And now I have."

"But it's not the same."

"No. We're both older. Wiser. We know what we want." He said it with purpose, let the words hang there in the air, and she was too cowardly to acknowledge them.

"I guess there's a reason why you're here at this time of the morning." She poured coffee into the mugs, handed him a cup.

"I was worried about you. I couldn't sleep." He shrugged, sipped the coffee, watching her over the rim.

"So, you drove all the way here to make sure I was okay?"

"I had some work to do at the office. I went there

first. Then came here. But you're really not far from my apartment. Only about twenty minutes."

"You said you've been back in San Antonio for a couple of years?" She sat at the table, split the muffin in two and held half out to Levi.

"I was in Austin for five years. Got offered a chance to transfer down here a little over two years ago."

"So, we've been living twenty minutes away from each other for two years and didn't even know it." She shook her head, wishing that everything she learned about Levi didn't fill her with regret. She'd come to terms with the woman she'd become since Aaron. She acknowledged that she would never be the light and easy spirit that she'd once been, but sitting across from Levi, looking into his eyes, she wished she could be the person he remembered.

"I guess it wasn't time for us to reconnect yet."

"Too bad." She took a bite of the muffin, choking it down past the lump in her throat.

"Why do you say that?"

"I'm not the person I was when we were kids. Not the person I was two years ago."

"And you think that matters to me?"

"I think it matters to *me*."

"If I had never known you when we were kids, I'd still be sitting here sharing this muffin with you. I'd still look into your eyes and wish I could take away the sadness I see there."

"Don't—"

"Don't say what I feel?"

"Don't pin a bunch of hopes and dreams on us. They're bound to get crushed." She started to stand, but he grabbed her hand, holding her in place.

"I'd rather have my dreams crushed then never have them at all." He lifted her hand, turning it palm up and pressing his lips to the scar there.

Warm lips.

Gentle touch.

Heat unfurling in her belly, something she thought dead springing to life again.

"Levi—"

"Don't ask me not to care." His lips traveled along the length of the scar, and he lifted his head, met her eyes. "Because I do, and there's no changing that."

"I'm not ready for this." But her heart pulsed with longing, her body shouting that this was Levi.

Levi.

The boy she'd grown up with. The one she'd loved from the first time she saw him.

Her best childhood friend.

Her first teenage crush.

She blinked back tears, pulled away from him. "I need to go get ready for church. Thanks for the muffin."

"Did you think I was leaving?" He settled back into his chair, watching through hooded eyes.

"Yes."

"I'm here to escort you to church, Susannah. Remember our deal? You're either at work or at home or with me."

"Church doesn't start for another couple of hours."

"Then there's no rush for you to get ready, and I have plenty of time to finish the other muffin." He pulled it from the bag, smiling as Susannah scowled.

"You were holding out on me."

"You never asked if I'd brought two. Besides, you didn't even eat your first half."

He was right. She'd left most of it crumbled on her plate.

"I didn't think I was hungry."

"And now that I have an entire muffin to myself, you are? Maybe you haven't changed as much as you think. You always did want everything I had." He broke a piece off his muffin, held it out, and she remembered a hundred Sunday afternoons, sitting on his back porch, begging him for candy or fruit or whatever snack he was eating. Remembered the amused tolerance in his face as he'd shared.

"I'm surprised you didn't ever tell me no." She took the muffin, let the sweetness melt on her tongue and chase away the bitter taste of regret.

"How could I? You stole my heart when I was ten and I saw you staring out the window of your parents' house, all wild hair and green eyes. There wasn't anything I wouldn't have done for you."

"Wish I'd have known that then. I would have demanded more." She smiled, tried to lighten the mood.

"You were never demanding, Susannah. You were just adoring. A heady thing for any boy."

"But you're not a boy anymore, and I'm not a five-year-old girl."

"And yet, I still can't resist you." He popped the last bite of muffin into his mouth and carried his plate to the sink. "I'm going out to my car to make a few phone calls. I'll be out there if you need me."

"You don't have to leave."

"If I stay, we're going to start talking about things you don't want to discuss. If I stay, I'm not going to pretend that I don't want to give you a lot more than a piece of muffin." He left before she could respond, walking out of the kitchen, out of the house, leaving her alone.

She wanted to call him back.

Wanted to tell him that as much as he still couldn't resist her, she still needed him. The way she had when the neighborhood bully had chased her home. The way she had when she'd broken her wrist jumping on the trampoline in his backyard. The way she had when she was learning to navigate school and friends.

The way she always had.

The way she still did.

She wanted to tell him that, but she wasn't as brave as Levi. She wasn't as certain of herself and her feelings.

She walked into her room, grabbing the clothes she'd pulled out before he'd called and showering quickly. No amount of water could wash away the compelling feel of his lips on her hand. No time alone could wipe away the memory of his words.

I still can't resist you.

And she couldn't resist him.

That was the truth.

The other truth was that she was terrified, her mind filled with ugly memories that had burned their way into her soul, tainted her forever. She shuddered, grabbing a soft sweater from her closet and pulling it on over her pencil skirt and fitted sweater.

The sun would be up soon. A new day to try to do what her family and friends insisted she needed to do and move forward. Away from the memories and the fear and the nightmares and into whatever God had planned.

"If only I knew what that was," she whispered, walking to the window, looking out into the blue-black morning.

Looking into a face.

Masked.

Features distorted by nylon.

A knife held in a gloved hand.

A nightmare come to life.

She screamed, jumping back, falling in her haste. Her head hit the corner of the dresser, but she barely felt it. Barely felt anything but her own pounding fear.

Up. Get up!

The order screamed through her mind, and she obeyed, jumping to her feet, screaming again, the sound filled with a million terrors, a thousand memories.

Out into the hall. Into the living room. Still screaming as she barreled into Levi, felt his arms wrap around her, his hand press her head to his chest.

"Susannah! What is it? What's wrong?" His voice was calm, his heart beating rapidly beneath her ear.

"Aaron."

"What?"

"In the backyard."

"Stay here!" He gently pushed her into a chair, ran into the kitchen. She heard the back door open. Close.

And she was alone again.

TEN

Levi pulled his cell phone from his pocket, calling in for backup as he raced into the yard. The morning was silent and still, but danger hung in the air.

He felt it.

A twig snapped. Another. Someone moving quickly, almost silently, and Levi followed, easing around the side of the house as a car engine sprang to life.

He sprinted to the front yard, nearly knocking Susannah over as she raced down the porch stairs.

"What are you doing out here? I told you to stay in the house!" he shouted, his arm hooked around her waist as he pulled her away from the fleeing vehicle.

"This is my battle. I can't let you fight it for me."

"That's what you said yesterday, and I bought into it, but this time, I'm going into battle with a gun, and you're going in dressed in a skirt and a pink sweater. One of us doesn't belong," he growled.

"We need to call the police." She ignored his comment.

"I already called for backup. They should be here soon. Did you see the car?"

"Yes. An old Mitsubishi. Dark blue or black. Pretty beat-up. It had a dent in the front fender."

"That matches what I saw. Go in the house and wait for my coworkers to show up. Anderson Michaels and Daniel Riley. Don't let anyone else in the house."

"Where are you going to be?"

"Hunting."

"You can't go after him alone!"

"We don't have time to waste arguing, Susannah. Go back in the house. Wait for my buddies. Give them a description of the car and the direction it was traveling."

"No."

"Susannah—"

"Let's go." She nearly ran to his car, pulled open the door he'd left unlocked when he'd decided to go back in her house for a second cup of coffee. When he'd heard her scream.

For as long as he lived, he didn't think he'd ever forget the sound of her terror. His hand shook as he shoved keys into the ignition. Shook with rage, with fear.

He'd been at her house to protect her, and he'd left her vulnerable and alone.

"It looks like your friends are here," she said as a black truck sped into view, emergency lights flashing in the window.

Levi pulled up beside it, lowering his window and meeting Anderson's concerned gaze. "We're searching for a dark Mitsubishi. Probably ten years old. Dent in the front bumper. Heading north."

"License plate number?"

"None that I could see."

"I'll have Ben issue an APB. What about the perp? Do you have a description?"

"Susannah?" He turned to her, and she shook her head, her hair flying, her eyes hollow with fear.

"He was wearing a nylon mask and gloves, carrying a knife. It looked..." Her voice trailed off, and Levi put a hand on her shoulder.

"Say what you're thinking. It'll be something to go on."

"It looked like the knife Aaron used. A butcher knife. About seven inches long. A black handle."

Anderson whistled but didn't comment, his gaze jumping from Levi to Susannah. He knew the story, and the pity in his gaze was exactly what Susannah had said she didn't want Levi to feel.

The pity he *wouldn't* feel.

For her sake.

"Let's go." He rolled up the window, pulled out

in front of Anderson's car, calling Daniel with a description of the car as he drove. Seconds later, Daniel's truck pulled up beside his. Three good guys. One bad guy.

The odds were improving, and Levi smiled grimly, offering Daniel a brief salute as he pulled ahead.

Dawn bathed the world in eerie light, casting shadows across yards and along driveways. The neighborhood was still asleep, houses dark and cars idle. Levi checked each one, searching for the Mitsubishi, praying he'd find it.

"He was heading toward the highway. If he makes it there, we'll never find him." Susannah leaned forward, her body still trembling slightly.

"With an APB out on his car, there isn't much chance he'll avoid detection on the highway. It's these back roads I'm worried about. Neighborhood streets. Driveways. There are plenty of places he could ditch the car and plenty of places to hide if he did."

"I think that's the car."

"Where?" Levi eased off the accelerator, searching the street.

"Down the road we just passed. It was parked in a driveway."

"You're sure?"

"Of course I am." Her confidence gave Levi hope. They had to find the car, had to find its driver, had to put an end to the cat-and-mouse game that had been playing out for months.

His cell phone rang as he coasted by a tiny ranch, his gaze on the Mitsubishi parked in its driveway. Dark blue. Beat-up. Old. It looked like the car he'd seen racing from Susannah's house.

He parked a few houses down, grabbing his cell phone as he studied the vehicle.

"Hello."

"Levi? It's Oliver Drew." Drew's boisterous voice filled the line. A member of Company D, he'd been spending extra hours pursuing leads and trying desperately to find the man who'd killed Gregory. It hadn't seemed to tire him. Even after he'd been poisoned while guarding Quin Morton, Oliver had been determined to be part of the investigation.

"What's up?"

"Cantana is playing games."

"What kind of games?" Doctor Jorge Cantana was a member of the Lions of Texas. Convicted of murdering restaurateur Axle Hudson, Cantana had refused to talk about the organization he belonged to and refused to admit any part in the murder of Gregory Pike.

"He had his lawyer call to say he was ready to talk. I went down to interview him, and he had nothing to say."

"How about we talk about what that means later? I have a situation I need to deal with."

"More Alamo trouble?"

"Looks like it. Call Ben. Tell him I have a vehicle that will need to be impounded for evidence." He rattled off the address, then texted the information to Daniel and Anderson.

If he'd been alone, he would have gotten out of the car, gone to investigate.

He wasn't, and he stayed put, his fingers tapping the dashboard, his body humming with the need for action.

"You can go look. I'll stay here."

"Like you stayed in the house?"

"I'll stay. We need to find this guy. We need to stop whatever all this is leading to. You sitting here babysitting me is getting in the way of that."

She was right.

He knew she was, and he opened the door, pulled his gun as he moved toward the car.

Empty.

No sign of a driver.

He covered his hand with the sleeve of his jacket, pressed it to the hood.

"Still warm?" Daniel got out of his truck, and Levi nodded.

"Yes."

"And you're sure this is the vehicle?"

"Same dented bumper. No license plate. Yeah. I'm sure."

"Looks like our guy fled. I'm going to call in a

canine unit. See if we can track him on foot. Why don't you take your friend back to her place? Ben's there. Said there's a knife in the backyard."

"I'd rather check out the car. See if the perp left anything behind."

"The Lions of Texas aren't big on leaving evidence."

"But they've made mistakes. All the members we've thrown in jail prove it."

"All the guys who aren't talking, you mean?"

"The border patrol agent and the sheriff that Gisella and Brock picked up confirmed what we thought about the Alamo celebration and The Lions' plans for it. And then there's Morton. He's their biggest mistake of all." Levi peered in the driver's side window, eyeing the dark interior.

"A mistake they've tried to rectify."

"Without success. Which brings me back to my point. They make mistakes. We're going to take them down for it."

"And take down Greg's killer while we're at it," Daniel muttered, pulling on gloves and opening the driver's door. "Looks clean."

"The glove compartment?"

"Empty."

"So, this was planned carefully."

"To what end? To chase your friend away from the Alamo? Seems like a waste of energy. She's one person. One security guard. Not much in the grand scheme of our defense measures." Daniel gestured to Levi's car and to Susannah who sat with her head back, her eyes closed. A dark smudge marred her forehead. Dirt? A bruise?

Levi frowned. "But a big deal if she's standing in the way of an Alamo Ranger aiding The Lions."

"True."

"I'd better take her back to her place. See what Ben has to say."

"I'll call you once the canine teams are done, or when we find or guy. Whichever comes first."

"Thanks."

Levi walked to his car, slid behind the steering wheel, his movement jostling the car. Susannah didn't move. Just stayed where she was. Eyes closed. Skin a shade too pale, the smudge on her forehead green and black and deep purple.

A bruise, but not a terrible one.

Nothing compared to the scar on her hand or the one peeking out from beneath the v-neck of her sweater. He ran his finger along the top edge of her collarbone, feeling the raised flesh of the scar. Another deep stab wound. One she'd been fortunate to survive.

He frowned, touching the bruise on her forehead, and she reared up, her eyes wide with fear, her fist swinging toward his face.

"Whoa!" He barely stopped the forward momentum, his hand wrapping around hers, pulling it down as she blinked, her green eyes still misty with sleep.

"What's going on?"

"You dozed off."

"Not the best time to do it," she said, her gaze jumping to the Mitsubishi.

"You were safe, and that's as good a time as any to sleep."

"Not when a criminal is escaping." She glanced out the car window and frowned. "He wasn't in the car?"

"No. Daniel is going to work with a canine team to try to track the guy. Ben is over at your place gathering evidence."

"Did he find anything?"

"A knife."

"I guess the guy wanted to make sure I knew he was really there."

"Either that, or he dropped it while he was running." Levi pulled out onto the road.

"Why run? That's what I keep wondering. He was standing right outside my window, Levi. He could have smashed the window and been in the house in minutes."

"Scare tactics."

"I hope you're right."

"What else could it be?"

"Nothing."

"What?" He pulled into her driveway, shifted in his seat so he was facing her.

"What if Aaron isn't dead? What if someone made a mistake and he's still alive? Still waiting to finish what he started last summer?" She shivered, and he pulled off his jacket, wrapped it around her shoulders.

"You know that isn't possible, right? The police identified him through fingerprints and dental records." Levi had double-checked the information the previous night.

"I know. It's just…too many memories, I guess." She brushed a strand of hair from her forehead, wincing as her fingers met bruised flesh. "I hit my head harder than I thought when I fell into the dresser."

"I was wondering how you got that. And this." His finger skimmed over the scar on her collarbone and she stilled.

"Same place I got the one on my palm, but you knew that."

"I was hoping I was wrong."

"It was bad, Levi. Worse than I want to talk about. I almost died, and that made me realize that I wanted to live every moment of every day like tomorrow wasn't going to come. And I'm trying, but all this stuff…the fear and the worry and the nightmares. They get in my way."

"I understand."

"I'm glad one of us does." She got out of the car, and he didn't try to stop her.

What could he say?

That things would get better in time?

That the fear and terror and memories would fade?

All those things were true, but until Levi found the person who was taunting Susannah, none of them mattered. The nightmare she'd escaped from was still going on. Would continue until the Lions of Texas were dismantled.

And they would be.

Levi had been gunning for them since Greg's death.

Now he had even more reason to take them down.

Between his efforts and the efforts of the rest of Company D, there was no doubt it would happen.

In time.

But that wasn't something they had much of, and he could feel it ticking away as he got out of the car and followed Susannah across the yard.

ELEVEN

Having one Texas Ranger in her kitchen had been bad enough, but two took up way more space than Susannah was comfortable with. She skirted around Captain Ben Fritz, poured coffee for him and for Levi, wishing they'd move the meeting into the living room. At least in there, she'd have room to breathe.

"Cream and sugar are on the counter. Help yourselves," she offered, as she handed each man a cup. Did either notice the way her hands were trembling? The way her voice shook?

Everything she'd said to Levi had been true.

She wanted to embrace every moment of every day.

But that was difficult to do with a predator chasing after her.

She shivered, pulling the edges of Levi's jacket more closely around her chest.

"Still cold?" Levi put down his coffee and rubbed

her arms, the brisk motion doing little to ease the chill that had settled deep into Susannah's soul.

"I'm okay. Thanks." She stepped back, knocking into a chair, her cheeks heating as Captain Fritz offered a sympathetic smile.

"Why don't you have a seat, Ms. Jorgenson? This won't take much time, and then you can go on with your day."

"I'm fine. Really." And if she said it enough maybe she'd convince herself of the fact.

"We've done some research on Aaron Simons. There's nothing to indicate he had any involvement with the Lions of Texas or in drug trafficking. Does that coincide with your knowledge of him?"

"Yes. He had high moral ideals."

"He tried to kill you. What kind of moral ideal allows for that?" Levi growled the question that Susannah had been asking herself for months. She'd found no answer. Couldn't bring the Aaron who'd been a counselor at Christian youth camp, who'd volunteered at homeless shelters, who'd led men's Bible studies into alignment with the other Aaron. The one who'd stalked her. Attacked her. Would have killed her.

"I don't know. I only know what I observed. He didn't smoke, didn't drink, never swore. He lived an upright life."

"An upright life that hid a black soul," Captain Fritz intoned, and Susannah nodded. "So, no involvement with The Lions, but someone who knows you *is* involved with them."

"It seems that way."

"You said the knife the guy was carrying tonight matched the one Aaron used?"

"It looked exactly the same."

"I have it here. Want to take a closer look?" He pulled a plastic bag from his evidence kit. Tagged with a number, sterile-looking but for the knife it contained.

Susannah's pulse leaped at the sight, her breath catching as she tumbled back in time, fell into her nightmare. Knife slashing. Blood pouring.

"Sit down, Susie. Before you fall down." Levi's tone was gruff, his hands gentle as he pushed her into a chair. He stayed behind her, his fingers brushing ends of her hair as Captain Fritz passed the bag across the table.

"It looks exactly the same."

"So we can assume that the person who brought it knew the kind of knife Aaron used."

"I guess so."

"Any idea who might have that information?"

"Anyone who watches the news. They flashed pictures of it every night for a week. Every time I saw it, I wanted to scream." She stood, walking away from the table, the knife.

If only it were as easy to walk away from the memories.

"Offhand, are there any Alamo Rangers who you

think could be bought? Maybe someone with financial troubles? Someone who feels he's owed more than what he's been given?"

"All the Rangers are vetted, Captain Fritz."

"Understood, but I'm not asking about vetting. I'm asking about your gut thoughts."

"Marcus Portman has a wife who's been in and out of the hospital for the last couple of months. He mentioned that medical bills are piling up. Other than that, I don't know anything about the finances of the people I work with."

"You don't spend time together outside of work?"

"No."

"What can you tell me about the perpetrator, Susannah? Height, weight, features?"

Susannah gave him the information as succinctly as she could, resisting the urge to point out similarities between the man looking in her window and Aaron. There were plenty of men with the same lean build. Plenty of men with the same height.

By the time the interview was over and Captain Fritz left, she felt drained, her head pounding with fatigue as she watched his Jeep disappear from sight.

"You all right?" Levi stood behind her, not touching her, not even close to touching, but she felt his presence as surely as she felt the warm sun on her face.

"I will be."

"It's just a few more days. That's all you have to make it through. Then this will be over. The Alamo anniversary celebration will be in the past." His hands wrapped around her waist and he pulled her back into his chest. Firm muscles pressed against her shoulders, his chin brushing her hair.

She let herself lean back, let him support some of her weight as she closed her eyes, inhaled spicy aftershave and Levi.

And it felt so much like coming home.

"What are you thinking?"

She shivered, but didn't have the strength to move away.

"That being here with you feels…good."

"Yeah? I was thinking the same thing."

"No, you weren't." She laughed lightly, turning in his arms, looking into his eyes.

"Then what *was* I thinking?"

"Probably deep thoughts about knives and Lions and drug trafficking. Probably even deeper thoughts about how to keep trouble away from the opening ceremony at the Alamo."

"You're wrong. I wasn't thinking about any of those things." He pressed his lips to her forehead, his hands sliding up her back, cupping her neck.

"Oh."

"I was thinking that I could stand here with you forever. That if this was the last moment of the last day of my life, I'd be happy to spend it with you."

"Levi—"

"We've come full circle, Susie. First together. Then apart. Now together again, and I'm thinking that's because this is the right time for us. The right place." His lips traced a line from her temple, to her cheek, to the corner of her mouth.

"Levi—"

"If you want me to stop, I will. If you want me to leave you alone, I'll do that, too. But I won't stop caring about you. Not this time around. You were in my heart when we were kids, and I'm beginning to think you never left it." His lips hovered over hers, and she wanted to tell him to stop, wanted to pull him close.

And somehow she was leaning in, feeling the warmth of his lips pressed to hers, the heat of his body seeping through her sweater. Her hands clutched his waist, her body humming with awareness. No nightmares. No fears. Just Levi.

"Probably we should stop," he mumbled against her neck, his lips finding the tender spot behind her ear.

"Probably." But it felt so right to be standing there with him, so right to slide her arms around his waist and hold on tight.

"When does church start?" The question registered through the dreamy haze Susannah had fallen into, and she pulled back, glanced at her watch.

"A half hour."

"Then we should probably get going."

"Right." She took a deep breath, stepped out of Levi's arms. "I'll get my Bible."

"You don't sound all that thrilled about it."

"It just gets tiring sometimes." She led him through the house, grabbed her Bible from her bedroom.

"Church?"

"Pretending that I'm okay. That everything is just like it used to be."

"Why would you do that?"

"Because the church I attend is filled with people I've known since I was a kid. They don't want to see me hurting, and I don't want them to worry."

"You still attend Faith Christian Church?"

"Yes."

The same church. With the same people. People who all wanted her to just be Susannah again. Sweet and happy and vibrant Susannah. She'd been told that so many times in the past few months that she thought she might drown in it.

"How about your folks?"

"Moved to Arizona a few years ago. My brother is there. He got married. Had a couple of kids, and they wanted to be closer to their grandchildren."

"They were great people." He held the car door open, waiting while she got in.

"They still are. They just don't live as close to me as they used to."

"Did they come back—"

"Last summer? Yes." She cut him off, not wanting to hear Aaron's name. Not wanting the thought of what had happened to mar the beauty of the morning, the peace she felt sitting in Levi's car.

"It must have been nice to have them around."

"They hovered, but I was glad. I needed that then."

"But not now?"

"Now, I just need people to forget."

"That may take a while."

"It may take a lifetime." She sighed as they pulled into the parking lot of Faith Christian Church. "You remembered where it was."

"How could I forget? I spent every Sunday of my childhood here. Now I'm attending a church closer to my apartment, but I'm suddenly remembering just what was so special about this place." He took her hand, and she didn't bother trying to pull away. Walking into church with Levi felt as right as stepping into his arms.

That should scare her. It should make her want to run the other way, but all she could do was walk down the hall, shoulder to shoulder with the man who'd once been the boy she'd loved.

"Susannah? Susannah Jorgenson! Hold it right there, my girl. I can't walk as fast as I used to."

Susannah dropped Levi's hand like it was a hot poker, blushing as she turned to face Charlotte

Calgary. The oldest member of the congregation, Charlotte was as much a part of the church as the hand-hewn wood floors and scuffed wooden pews.

"Good morning, Ms. Charlotte." Susannah greeted her with a gentle hug.

"It is, my dear, but you're running a little late for service. I hope you didn't have any trouble last night. I heard there were problems at the Alamo, and I've been worried about you."

"Who did you hear that from?"

"My niece works for the sheriff's office. She said there was a bomb scare."

"We did find a package on the premises, and the bomb squad was called, but it turned out to be nothing."

"Thank goodness. I'd hate for anything to happen there just a few days before the big celebration."

"Me, too."

"Have you heard that the vice president will be here?"

"Yes."

"And the governor. It really is just so wonderful!" She hurried away, and Susannah watched her go.

"What's wrong?" Levi nudged Susannah toward the sanctuary.

"Just thinking that Zarvy won't be happy to know that the bomb threat is no longer a secret."

"It never was. He should have known better than

to try to keep it from the media. Word of mouth can spread information just as quickly as the news."

"Maybe we can use that to our advantage."

"What do you mean?" Levi paused with his hand on the closed sanctuary door, his gaze dropping to her lips for a heartbeat. Her pulse responded, leaping up. Jumping with joy.

"Captain Fritz seems convinced that an Alamo Ranger is working for the Lions."

"It makes sense."

"I wish it didn't, but I can't argue. So, maybe we just start asking around, talking to people that know my coworkers. Someone, somewhere knows something. We just have to find out who."

"It's a good plan, Susie, but our time is limited. I'm not sure we'll be able to cast our net wide enough to reel anything in."

"We can't just wait around for him to strike again."

"We won't. I'm going to set up interviews with your coworkers. We'll see who's willing to take a lie detector test and who isn't, and we'll go from there."

"It just seems like we should be doing more."

"My office has been working overtime for months. We're doing all that we can, and I know that your people are doing the same. When are you scheduled to work next?"

"Marcus asked me to take his shift for a few

hours tomorrow morning. I'm also working tomorrow night."

"Just what I thought."

"What?"

"We have a long week ahead of us. We need to take some time to recharge." He opened the sanctuary door, his fingers brushing Susannah's back as she walked past, his warmth seeping through her, stealing her anxiety away.

A long week?

It had been a long few months, but settling into a pew next to Levi, his arm pressed to hers, Susannah could almost believe there was an end in sight. Could almost believe that she and Levi really had come full circle, and that this really was their time.

TWELVE

Three in the morning wasn't a good time to be awake.

It was an even worse time to be walking from her car to the Alamo. Dark shadows stretched across the road, chasing Susannah as she hurried across the street. Just a few more feet and she'd be inside the compound. A few more seconds and she'd be safe.

Something scuffled on the pavement behind her, the sound making her blood run cold. She didn't want to look. Didn't want to face whatever was behind her. Then again, she'd rather face death head-on than die with her back to it.

She swung around, her heart leaping when she saw a man moving along the sidewalk a dozen yards away. Briefcase in hand, focused straight ahead, he moved with a purposeful stride, going to prepare for an early-morning meeting or heading into the office to get an early start on the day. Nothing on his mind but the job.

That's the way Susannah wanted to be. Focused on the task, not afraid of what lurked in the shadows. Confident of herself and her surroundings.

Obviously, she had a long way to go before she got to that.

She took off her hat, ran a hand over her hair. *A long week ahead.* That's what Levi had said, and Susannah had no doubt he was right. Six days until the opening ceremony to launch the celebration of the 175th anniversary of the Battle of the Alamo. Six days to make sure that whatever the Lions had planned wouldn't come to fruition.

It wasn't a lot of time to come up with answers.

She unlocked the chapel door, calling out as she entered the dark building. "Hello? Anyone here?"

"Me. I'm in the office wondering if I'm going to die of boredom or hunger first." Jeremy Camp appeared in the office doorway, his hangdog expression making Susannah smile.

"No action tonight, huh?" She poured a cup of coffee, then dumped cream and sugar into it.

"Not even a cat running through the courtyard."

"That's good news, right?"

"Not if a man wants to stay awake, but I suppose quiet nights are good for the Alamo."

"They'll make the Alamo Planning Committee and Chad happy, anyway."

"Guess as long as we make it through the next

few days without any trouble, we'll all be happy. I don't know about you, but this change in the schedule is eating into my social life."

"It'll be over soon enough. Who pulled shift with you?"

"Luke Bristol. He's out doing final rounds. We'll take off when he gets here, and then it'll be you and..." He lifted a sheet of paper and frowned. "You're not scheduled until tonight. You know that?"

"I'm filling in until Marcus can get here."

"More trouble with his wife?"

"I'm afraid so."

"Too bad." He didn't sound like he thought it was, and something passed behind his eyes. Irritation or dislike.

"He can't help that his wife is having pregnancy complications."

"I guess not, but he's never been consistent, even before his wife's troubles."

"What do you mean?"

"Just what I said. You don't pull shifts enough with him to know it, but he misses a couple of days a month." He shrugged, grabbed a jacket from the back of a chair and put it on.

"I'm sure he has good reasons."

"His reasons don't matter to me, Susannah. We sign on and agree to work when we're scheduled. Seems to me, we should work. But maybe I'm just old-fashioned. How long will you be here?" He changed the subject, and Susannah wondered if there were more he could say. She'd mentioned Marcus to Captain Fritz, but she hadn't really believed he could be capable of working for The Lions.

Then again, she didn't want to believe any of her coworkers were capable of that.

"Just a few hours. Who am I working with?" She glanced at the schedule, frowning when she saw that the name next to Marcus's had been crossed out. "Sara's not coming in?"

"She told Chad she wouldn't be able to. She'll pull a double tomorrow to make up for it."

"So, who's coming?" *Please, please let someone be coming.* She did *not* want to work the shift alone.

"Don't know. Chad said he'd arrange it. So, someone will be here." He paused, eyed her with a mixture of pity and concern. "You know, I can stick around for a while if you want. Make sure the replacement shows up. That way—"

"And have you blame me for your less-than-impressive social life? I don't think so." She kept her voice light, forced herself to smile. Forced herself to be the woman she'd once been, happy and relaxed and excited.

"You sure?"

No.

"Of course I'm sure."

"All right, then. I'm heading out. Supposed to go over to Texas Rangers headquarters later today. Get myself polygraphed. I'd better rest up before then. Wouldn't want fatigue to throw the test off."

"You're having a polygraph test?" If so, the Rangers were working quickly, moving forward with Levi's plan.

"I'm not the only one. They asked Luke to come in, too. I wouldn't be surprised if they asked everyone. Someone dropped that box off in front of the barracks. The video doesn't show anyone but our security team entering the compound. Makes sense that it was one of us."

"Any ideas who it might be?" she asked, her heart beating a little faster.

"Wish I did. Wouldn't mind being the hero of the hour. I'm going to radio Luke and tell him you're here. Bet he's as anxious to get out of here as I am. I'll see you tomorrow. We're working back-to-back shifts." He offered a quick salute and walked out of the office.

Susannah sipped her coffee, listening as Jeremy radioed Luke and let him know that their shift had ended. For a moment, the chapel was filled with sounds as Luke entered from the compound and the two men greeted each other. A door opened. Closed. A lock turned.

And she was alone.

She wanted to be okay with that.

She told herself she *was* okay with that.

But she couldn't shake the images that raced through her mind.

A knife.

A man outside her window.

Hard arms holding her down. A knife plunging toward her heart.

Blood pouring out as she ran, every nightmare she'd ever had chasing her.

"Enough!" She slammed her coffee down on the desk, the liquid splashing up onto her hand and splattering her shirt.

She grabbed a napkin, dabbed the spots half-heartedly.

She just needed Marcus to hurry up. She needed whoever was running shift with her to hurry up. She needed the sun to rise, the nightmares to fade.

Something scraped against the chapel door. A key against the lock. Someone opening the door.

Her partner for the next few hours?

Or the man who'd stood outside her window with a knife in her hand?

She fumbled through her purse, pulled out pepper spray and a pen. She'd been trained in self-defense. She knew what to do and how to do it, but that hadn't helped her when Aaron attacked. He'd been enraged, his anger fueling a strength that had been beyond anything Susannah was prepared for.

If she'd had her gun on her then, she would have used it. Now she kept it holstered, afraid she might pull the trigger without cause.

Fear did that to people. Made them trigger-happy and too quick to act.

Feet tapped on the tile floor outside the office, and Susannah tensed. She wanted to dive behind a desk, hide from whoever was coming, but she hurried across the room instead, stepping out of the office and straight into Levi.

Relief flooded through her, and she sagged against him, his arms wrapping around her waist. "Levi! What are you doing here?"

"Working my shift."

"Shift?"

"I told Chad I'd fill in where he needed me. Ben has assigned a few other Rangers to do the same."

"That will help."

"Let's hope so." His gaze dropped from her face to her hand, and his lips quirked into a smile. "Were you expecting someone else?"

"Just being careful."

"Your gun would do more damage." He took the pepper spray, turned it over in his hand.

"I know."

"But?" One hand still rested on her waist, his touch light and easy and undemanding.

"I'm too jumpy, and I'm afraid I'll pull the trigger by mistake." The truth slipped out and heat stained her cheeks.

"You'd never shoot unless it was necessary, Susannah. I'm sure of that."

"I'm glad one of us is." She moved away, the imprint of his hand still searing her side.

And she craved more. More contact. More comfort. More of the feeling of being safe and cherished.

"I could take you to a firing range. We could shoot a few rounds together. Maybe that'll make you feel more comfortable."

"I've had a gun for four years, and I've never felt uncomfortable until now. Shooting at targets seven days a week can't keep me from pulling a trigger too quickly."

"So you carry a gun and shoot pepper spray?" He frowned, handing her the container.

"It's effective."

"Unless your attacker takes it from you before you get a chance to use it."

"Thanks, Levi. That makes me feel so much more comfortable." She shoved the repellent into her pocket.

"If I wanted to make you comfortable, I'd tell you that I don't think you have to worry about carrying anything. I'd tell you that what happened yesterday morning was a fluke and that I don't think you're in danger."

"I *shouldn't* be in danger. I *shouldn't* have anything to worry about."

"Maybe you're not. Maybe you don't. We haven't established much of anything. Just that someone wants to scare you. It still pays to be cautious."

"I heard you've scheduled lie detector tests for some of the Alamo Rangers."

"I figured there was no time like the present to get started."

"The two men who worked shift before me seem willing to cooperate."

"Someone won't be. I feel pretty confident of that."

"I wish I knew who. That would save us a lot of effort and time."

"Time we don't have."

"It does seem to be ticking away quickly, doesn't it?" She put her coffee cup down and stretched.

"Still tired?"

"Exhausted."

"The bruise on your head looks better." He pushed her hat up a little higher, pressing a finger to the still-tender flesh.

"Well, it doesn't feel better, so you can stop poking at it." She stepped back, but it wasn't the pain that was getting to her. It was Levi. His heat, his scent, his pure masculinity, they seemed to sink into her skin, stay there.

"Sorry about that. I didn't mean to hurt you."

"You didn't."

"You're sure?" He bent close, his breath fanning across her cheek as he studied the bruise, and something deep in her belly sprang to life.

"Yes." Her breath caught as she looked into his eyes, her pulse jumping.

"Good, because if you were still hurt, I couldn't do this." He kissed her cheek. "Or this." His lips blazed a trail of fire from cheek to chin to lips, and Susannah swayed, her hands pressed against his chest for balance, her heart thrumming a quick, light beat.

"This isn't a good idea." She stepped back, pressed her fingers to her lips as if that could change what had happened.

Two days. Two kisses.

And no matter how much she knew she should, she couldn't regret them.

"Maybe you're right, but I find you hard to resist, Susie."

"You resisted me for nine years. I think you can resist me for a while longer."

"Touché." He chuckled and walked out of the office. "How about we go run patrol for a while?"

"Sure." She followed him out into the compound, the darkness not nearly as dark when he was with her. "Any new developments in the case?"

"The car was clean. No fingerprints. No papers. Nothing. The knife was the same way."

"I guess that means we're no closer to finding the answers we need."

"No, and we're going to be explaining that to the Alamo Planning Committee this afternoon."

"What do you mean?"

"Zarvy has called another meeting. This time, the entire committee will be there. He wants a full report on the bomb threat and our response to it."

"What time?"

"Two. Zarvy wanted to meet this morning, but you're working now and night shift, and I figured you'd want to get some sleep in between."

"I could have slept after the meeting."

"Not if Zarvy managed to stretch the meeting out for hours like he usually does."

"Let's hope he doesn't do that today. Our time is already limited. I hate to waste it sitting in on a meeting."

"I feel the same, but Zarvy is insisting."

"Hey! Hey!" A man's voice called from the darkness to their left, the sound of metal rattling against metal filling the night.

Filling Susannah with dread.

The gate.

Someone was at the gate.

A short, sharp scream.

Another harsh rattle.

And thick, pregnant silence.

"Stay here." Levi ran toward the gate, and Susannah followed. Not because she wanted to prove herself or her courage, but because the Alamo was her jurisdiction, the job of protecting it hers to fulfill. Her feet pounded on pavement, her pulse raced, but the fear she expected, the fear she dodged every moment of every day didn't come.

A dozen feet ahead, Levi skidded to a stop in front of the gate. "Do you have a key?"

"Yes." She pulled it out, adrenaline pumping through her, driving away everything but the need to act.

Just beyond the gate, streetlights fell on a crumpled figure. Dark liquid spilled from beneath his head, trickling out onto the pavement, staining it deep purple-black.

Blood. Lots of blood.

Running from hand and abdomen and throat.

No!

Susannah pulled her thoughts up short, refused to fall into the past. She ran forward, knelt on cool pavement.

"Sir?" But he was unresponsive, his neck turned at an unnatural angle. Was it broken?

Susannah lifted his wrist, felt a solid, steady pulse.

"Sir? Are you okay?" The man groaned, shifted so she could see his face.

"Mitch?" She frowned, the scent of alcohol and

sweat filling the air as he struggled to a sitting position. Blood oozed from a wound in his head, spilling down onto his shirt and dripping onto the pavement.

"What's goin' on? What's happening?" His words slurred together, and he wiped at the blood, smearing it across his forehead and cheek.

"We were wondering the same thing," Levi said, holding Mitch steady as he swayed and almost fell backward.

"You throwing me in jail, Ranger?"

"The only place I'm going to throw you is into an ambulance."

"Don't need an ambulance. I need to talk to Susie."

"You do need an ambulance. You can talk to me while you're waiting for it to arrive." She met Levi's eye, and he nodded, pulling out a cell phone and calling for help as she took off her jacket and pressed it against the wound in Mitch's head. "Hold this. You don't want to bleed to death before help arrives."

"Don't want to bleed to death after it arrives, either," he muttered, doing as she asked.

"Want to tell me how this happened?"

"That's what I need to say to you, Sus."

"What?"

"Watch your back. That crazy guy, he's comin' for you again. I tried to stop him, wanted to keep him here and call the police. Wanted to keep you safe. You've always treated me nice. Don't want anything to happen to ya." The drunken slur was gone, the dazed look replaced by a sharp stare.

"What crazy guy?" But she knew who he was talking about, and her blood ran cold, all her fear racing back until she was shaking with it.

Watch your back.

Edith Zarvy had said the same thing, and the warning lodged in her chest, filled her lungs.

"Him. The one who was coming around before. Only he's different this time." He tripped over the words, sagging forward. Levi caught him before he toppled over, easing him onto the pavement.

"Who, Mitch?" Levi leaned close, his words forceful and demanding, and Mitch blinked, looked at him as if he hadn't realized he was there.

"Don't know, but he's here. Saw him at the gate. Tried to stop him."

"Did you see his face?"

"No face. Told you. He's back. Guy who used to come around here looking for Susie. Guy who hurt her."

No face?

So, he'd been wearing a mask. Susannah met Levi's eyes, knew he was thinking what she was—that their perp had tried to enter the compound again.

Had he known Susannah was there? Or had he simply wanted to leave another message?

An ambulance shrieked toward them, its flashing lights illuminating the street, the pavement and the blood that pooled where Mitch's head had been. Seconds later, a marked police car appeared, lights flashing, sirens blaring. Help had arrived, and Susannah went through the motions, answered the questions, did everything she could to explain what Mitch had said and what she believed had happened. The officer dusted for prints that Susannah knew he wouldn't find. The EMTs checked Mitch's vitals and loaded him onto a stretcher, and all along, two words floated around in Susannah's head.

He's back.

They stayed there as she accepted the police officer's card. Stayed there as she scanned the area one last time, searching for someone watching from the shadows, hoping someone would be. They needed to find the guy responsible. They needed to stop him before someone else was hurt.

"You okay?" Levi stood beside her as the ambulance and police car sped toward the hospital. Mitch would be questioned there. Maybe he'd have more to offer. Probably he wouldn't. Between the knock on his head and the alcohol he'd been drinking, it was doubtful he'd have much of a memory of anything that had happened.

"Better than Mitch."

"He's a tough old guy. He'll be fine."

"He lost a lot of blood."

"Head wounds bleed a lot."

"That doesn't make me feel any better."

"What would?"

"Finding the guy who did it."

"We will."

"I don't mean in a day or two or a month. I mean now. This minute."

"It would be nice if it worked that way, but it doesn't. Finding the guy is going to take more legwork and more time."

"Time seems to be a hot commodity lately."

"Yeah. Come on. We need to go back in and secure the Alamo. Make sure that what happened to Mitch wasn't a diversionary tactic."

"You don't think the guy walked in through another gate while we were helping Mitch, do you?"

"No, but we need to check, anyway. Make sure things are secure. One explosive planted in just the right place—"

"Would take out the vice president, the governor and the lieutenant governor. I know. Trust me. There's no need to keep repeating it."

"Could take them out, but we're not going to let that happen." He linked fingers with her, tugging her away from the blood-soaked sidewalk and into the Alamo compound.

She went willingly.

Because she knew he was right. They needed to

secure the compound, needed to make sure it hadn't been breached while they were distracted.

And because she couldn't do anything else.

When they were kids, she'd idolized Levi. Made him bigger than life. A superhero.

Now, they were adults, and she saw him for who he was.

Not a superhero. Not bigger than life.

Better.

A man working hard to do the right thing. A man unwilling to compromise his principles and values. A man who'd fight for justice no matter the odds.

A man she could fall for if she let herself.

THIRTEEN

The compound was empty. Not a surprise. Levi hadn't been expecting Mitch's assailant to be hanging around.

He'd been hoping, though.

Hoping the mistakes the Lions had been making would cumulate into one big miscalculation.

Susannah's radio crackled, and a tinny voice filled the night. "Susannah, it's Marcus. Do you copy?"

"I copy. Glad you finally made it, Marcus. Is your wife doing okay?" She spoke into the radio, her stride lengthening as they approached the chapel.

"Better. Where are you?"

"Just coming into the chapel. We've had some trouble."

"Again?"

"Outside the gates this time, but close enough to matter."

"Did you call Chad?"

"I haven't had a chance."

"I'll give him a ring. I'm in the office when you get here."

"See you in a minute." She snapped the radio back into her belt as Levi held the chapel door open.

"Marcus didn't need you to cover his shift for very long, did he? What's it been? An hour and a half?"

"He was at the hospital with his wife last night. He wanted to go home and shower and change before reporting for duty."

"He couldn't have showered at the hospital?"

"It was probably more comfortable to do it at home. Besides, I didn't mind coming in for him. Now that he's here, I'm going to head to the hospital to see how Mitch is doing."

"How about you wait until I can go with you?"

"I'd rather not."

"And I'd rather you not be wandering around San Antonio without an escort. We had a deal, remember? You let me stick close, and I won't ask Chad to remove you from duty."

She scowled, but didn't argue.

Good.

He had no intention of compromising.

No intention of backing down.

"Susannah? Is that you?" Marcus hurried from the office, his dark hair spiked up around a sallow face.

"How's Deborah?" Susannah responded, moving forward to greet him.

"As good as can be expected. They're probably going to send her home tonight."

"That's good news."

"Yeah. It is. Doesn't seem like we're getting much good news around here, though. What happened?"

"You remember Mitch?" Susannah asked.

"The guy you found in the compound the other night? How could I forget?"

"Someone attacked him."

"What? Why?"

"We don't know."

Levi pulled out his phone while Susannah filled Marcus in on the details, moving into the office as he waited for Ben to answer.

"It's a little early for a phone call, so I'm going to assume something is wrong?" Ben growled, and Levi knew exactly how he felt. Frustrated. Tired of the game. Ready for it to be over.

"I'm afraid so."

"Another intruder?"

"No. An older guy was attacked outside the compound. He's been brought to the hospital. I was hoping you could have someone question him there."

"Gisella is off shift in a few minutes. I can send her to look for the guy. You have a name?"

"Just Mitch."

"I'm assuming you think this is connected to the Lions."

"I have no doubt."

"Want to explain?"

"The old guy was trying to warn Susannah about something. He took a pretty hard knock on the head, so we're not sure what he was trying to say."

"He and Susannah know each other?"

"Mitch makes it a habit of hanging out at the Alamo when he's drunk."

"Let's just make sure he doesn't crash the opening ceremony."

"I think that's the least of our worries."

"Agreed. I'm going to send Oliver to take your shift at the Alamo. I want you and Susannah to go to the hospital. From what you've said, I think Mitch will respond better to her than anyone else."

"Good call."

"I'll still send Gisella to check on him while you're waiting for Oliver, and I'll give you a call if his condition changes."

"Thanks."

"No problem. I'll see you at the meeting this afternoon."

"See you then."

Levi hung up. Only then did he notice the silence. Had Susannah left? Was she walking to her car unescorted?

"She'd better not be," he muttered as he surveyed the empty room.

"Better not be what?" Susannah walked out of the office, her hat off.

"Walking to your car alone."

"After what happened to Mitch, did you really think I would?"

"You walked here unescorted."

"How did you…?" She stopped, her eyes narrowing as she speared him with a look that would have made stronger men than Levi cower. "You were watching me."

"I watch lots of people. It's part of the job."

"What did you do? Wait outside my house all night and then follow me here?"

"When you say it like that, it doesn't sound like the best idea I've ever had." But it had made sense at the time. He'd known the perp would show himself again, and he'd been hoping to be around when it happened.

He'd also wanted to make sure Susannah was safe.

Things were escalating quickly, and he didn't want her to be caught in the cross fire between the Texas Rangers and the Lions of Texas.

"I'd like to say it was the worst idea you've ever had." She frowned, twirling her hair through her fingers in the same restless gesture he remembered from their childhood.

"But you won't?"

"Not if you don't say that walking from my car to the compound by myself was the worst idea *I've* ever had."

"It wasn't. Walking from here to your car alone? That might have been."

"Eventually, I'm going to have to leave. You know that, right? I mean, I can't stay here with you all morning."

"Too bad. I can think of a lot of interesting things we could do together," Levi said.

"How about you think of something else, because I'm done with interesting things."

"I was talking about marking out the stage area for the ceremony. I want to see exactly where the guests will be standing when they speak."

"Oh." She blushed, turning away as Marcus stepped out of the office.

"You two leaving?"

"I'm waiting for my replacement. Then we'll head out."

"All right. I'm going to do rounds. Use the radio if you need anything."

"You said you have a replacement coming?" Susannah asked, her gaze following Marcus as he left the chapel.

"Oliver Drew. He's a member of my company. Once he gets here, I'll drive you over to the hospital, and we'll see how Mitch is doing."

"Thanks." She smiled, the first real smile he'd seen all morning. He wanted to lean in, taste it on her lips.

"For what?"

"Not making me wait to visit Mitch. I've grown to care about him."

"Obviously, the feeling is mutual. He was determined to get that warning to you."

"I feel terrible that he was hurt in the process."

"Hopefully not too badly. I asked Ben to send a Ranger over to check on Mitch, so we should know the extent of his injuries soon."

A soft tap sounded on the chapel door, and Susannah pulled it open, allowing Oliver Drew to step into the room.

His gaze rested on Susannah briefly, and then landed on Levi. "Hey, McDonall. I hear you summoned me?"

"That was Ben, but thanks for coming."

"You're not going to thank me when I give you the news Ben sent me with."

"What news?"

"Gisella went down to the emergency room, looking for the guy who was beaten outside of the Alamo's gate. He's gone."

"Gone as in left the hospital? Or gone as in dead?" Levi asked.

"Left the hospital. I guess he didn't think he needed treatment."

"Or he was afraid if he stayed, he'd be a sitting duck. Just because he wasn't killed outside the compound, doesn't mean the person who struck him wasn't trying to murder him," Levi responded.

"Good point." Oliver smiled. "You must be Susannah."

"That's right."

"I'm Ranger Oliver Drew. I heard you've been keeping Levi busy."

"Actually, the Alamo is keeping him busy. We've had a lot of action these past few days."

"Maybe I'll see some of it while I'm here."

"I think Ben would prefer it if things stay quiet." Levi took Susannah's arm, walked toward the chapel door. "We're going to head out. Will you be at the Alamo Planning Committee meeting this afternoon?"

"If Ben wants me there. Personally, I'd as soon skip it."

"You and me both."

"Unfortunately, you don't have a choice." Oliver grinned as Levi walked outside.

The sun had yet to crest the horizon, and the sky was pitch-black. No moon. Thick clouds covering the stars. Not a good night to be wandering around with a head injury.

Where had Mitch gone?

A shelter?

Did he have family to stay with?

"I hope he's okay," Susannah said, her words barely carrying through the darkness.

"Mitch? I told you, he's a tough old guy. He'll be fine."

"Not if he didn't leave the hospital of his own volition. What if someone followed the ambulance to the hospital, walked into the emergency and—?"

"Kidnapped him? I have a feeling Mitch would have put up quite a fight."

"You're probably right."

"I know I'm right. It would have been easy enough for someone to sneak into the hospital, but it would have been nearly impossible for anyone to sneak Mitch out."

"I'm still worried about him." They stopped at her car, and Susannah leaned against the door, her face a pale oval, her eyes shadowed.

"I know. That's one of the things I've always loved about you. That you care so deeply." He hooked his thumb in her belt loop, pulled her a step closer.

"Levi—"

"Are you going to tell me this is a bad idea?"

"I don't know if it *is* a bad idea."

"Then how about we just take things slow, see how they play out?" He tugged her in so that her head was resting on his chest, smoothed his hand down her silky hair.

Slowly, her hands slid around his waist, and he

smiled, inhaling the sweet berry scent of her shampoo. "See? That's not so bad, is it?"

"No. It's just—"

"Levi! Hold up!" Oliver called out from across the street, his footsteps echoing through the darkness as he ran toward them.

"What's wrong?" Levi's hand dropped to his gun, as he stepped in front of Susannah, blocking her from an unseen threat.

"Nothing to get too riled up about. Ben just called. The meeting has been rescheduled."

"Sounds like good news to me."

"Rescheduled to happen now rather than this afternoon."

"It's not even dawn." Susannah stepped out from behind Levi and frowned.

"I think that's the point. There are some high-powered people in attendance. They don't want media coverage. Don't want anyone to know they're concerned about security details for the ceremony."

"Who are we talking about?" Levi asked.

"Besides the planning committee? Some of Governor Kingston's people and Senator Huffington."

"That puts a spin on things." President Pro Tem of the Texas Senate, Huffington was third in line to the governorship of Texas. He was also speaking at the opening ceremony.

"The meeting is at the Riverwalk Hotel. Penthouse suite."

"You're coming?"

"Unfortunately, I don't have a choice. They want as many of us there as possible."

"Us?"

"Security personnel. Ben's words, not mine."

"So, Marcus is alone at the Alamo?" Susannah stopped, and Levi was sure she planned to turn around and go back.

"He assured me he'd be fine until I got back. I can't see any reason why he wouldn't be. It seems all the incidents at the Alamo center around you."

Susannah visibly stiffened at Oliver's words, but she didn't respond.

There wasn't much she could say. Wasn't much Levi could say, either.

Everything that was happening seemed to be centered around Susannah and the Alamo.

The Lions' agenda. Levi felt confident of that.

He only wished he knew what that agenda was. Why they wanted Susannah out of the way. What they hoped to accomplish at the opening ceremony.

Time.

Ticking away.

The ceremony was just a few days away, and they had more questions than answers. More trouble than peace. If he had his way, Levi would gladly put Susannah on a plane and fly her to another state, hide her away until Greg's killer was in custody and the Lions of Texas had been destroyed.

But he couldn't have his way.

All he could do was stick close to her side and pray that that would be enough to keep her safe.

FOURTEEN

Ranger Oliver Drew was nothing like Levi.

The thought flitted through Susannah's mind as they walked to the Riverwalk Hotel. Levi's body was taut and hard, his stride brisk and confident. Oliver moved more slowly and with less purpose, his body softer, his stomach pushing against his pale yellow shirt.

He flashed Susannah a smile as they started across the street. "Don't look so nervous. No one there bites."

"I'm not worried about them biting, I'm worried about them firing me."

"For what?"

"I haven't exactly done a stellar job of keeping the Alamo secure."

"I don't think anyone could have done any better," Levi broke in, his words not as soothing as Susannah would have liked them to be.

Of course he thought she'd done a good job.

He was…

What?

Blinded by his feelings for her?

Old feelings.

New ones.

She understood.

She felt them, too, rising up and spilling out every time they were together.

"McDonall is right. You did as well as anyone could have."

"I appreciate you saying that, Ranger Drew."

"Call me Oliver. I'm not into formalities." He offered a smile, and Susannah tried to respond in kind, but her smile felt forced, faked, as stiff as a board, and she finally gave up the effort, her gaze on the stunning Riverwalk Hotel.

"I guess we're here."

"No need to sound so gloomy. It's not a death sentence, Susie." Levi's voice rumbled in her ear as they stepped into the opulent lobby and hurried toward a bank of elevators.

"Of course it's not," she said, but she wasn't sure she believed it. She'd worked hard to become an Alamo Ranger, and over the past few days, she'd begun to think that she could push past her fear, continue her job. If it was taken from her, her childhood dream would die.

Just as another was springing to life.

She glanced at Levi, her heart jumping as she met his eyes.

He was everything she remembered from their childhood.

More.

"You look pale, Susannah. Are you sure you're up to this? Me and McDonall can handle it if you'd like." Oliver's offer pulled her from her thoughts. Good thing. She had too many other things to worry about, too much to focus on. She couldn't afford to be distracted by anything.

Or anyone.

"You said they wanted as many security personnel as possible. Since I'm security personnel, I need to be there. Thanks for your concern, though."

"No problem. Guess we all should zip up our jackets. I think things are about to get really chilly," Oliver said as the elevator door opened into the hotel's penthouse suite.

A short, wiry man greeted them, checking their ID and then motioning them to a room to the left. The door was closed, a hushed murmur of voices carrying through as Levi knocked.

"Come!"

Susannah was first into the room, Levi and Oliver stepping aside so she could enter. A dozen pairs of eyes watched as she took a seat next to Chad. He smiled grimly, anger flashing in the depth of his eyes.

Not good.

Chad didn't lose his temper. He didn't get angry. If he was, things were worse than either of them had anticipated.

"Glad to see the security team is punctual. At least you've gotten that right." Hank Zarvy's tone set Susannah's teeth on edge, and she bit her lip to keep from falling into the trap she knew he was setting. If she became defensive, she'd lose the war before the first battle had even begun.

"Hank, let's not start this meeting off the wrong way." A pretty redhead spoke up, offering Susannah an easy smile. She looked familiar, but Susannah couldn't place her face.

"What's wrong with the way I'm starting it, Melora? We've had trouble left and right at the Alamo, and I want an answer as to why."

Melora?

An unusual name, and it sparked Susannah's memory. Melora Hudson's husband, Axle, had been missing for years, his body just recently discovered.

"There's always going to be trouble when big events like this are planned, and it isn't the fault of Alamo security."

"That's a matter of opinion." But Zarvy settled back into his seat, his gaze on Susannah.

"Well, my opinion agrees with Ms. Hudson's." A suave dark-haired man spoke up, rising from his position at the end of the table. Susannah had seen him on television plenty of times during his bid for senate, but Senator Huffington was even more compelling in person, his intense gaze touching on each person in the room before landing on Susannah.

"You're Susannah Jorgenson."

"That's right."

"Your supervisor has been telling us what an outstanding security officer you are. We appreciate that and don't want you to think this meeting is any reflection on your work."

She wasn't sure what he expected her to say, so she simply nodded, waiting for him to continue.

"Unfortunately, it's becoming clear that security at the Alamo isn't where it needs to be to guarantee Sunday's success. What we'd like to do during this meeting is establish alternate security in the form of Texas Rangers and Secret Service agents."

"They've already been included in the plans," Susannah offered, though she knew where he was heading. The planning committee planned to yank the Alamo out from under Alamo Ranger control.

"I think you're misunderstanding what Senator Huffington is saying. Your plans, whatever they may be, aren't working. We're going with Plan B," Zarvy spoke up.

"Which is?" Levi asked, a dangerous edge to his voice. Obviously, he was reading things the same way Susannah was.

"The Alamo Rangers will be present at the Alamo, but we're moving in a full security team. Twenty men and women handpicked to keep the site secure. They'll arrive this afternoon and be on-site until Sunday after the ceremony." Zarvy's smug announcement was met with a silence so thick Susannah thought she might choke on it.

Say something.

Say.

Something.

She cleared her throat, stood. "If I could have a few minutes of your time, maybe I can convince you that such extreme measures aren't necessary."

Every eye rested on her. Everyone in the room waited for her to speak.

Too bad she had no idea what to say.

"Go ahead, Ms. Jorgenson." Senator Huffington settled into his chair, tapping his fingers together impatiently.

Levi was to his left, his hat off, his hair slightly mussed, his brown eyes warm and welcoming. He smiled, and she relaxed, focusing her attention on Huffington as she explained the measures that had been put into place, gave details of the bomb scare, stressed the fact that there had never been any real danger and went over security details for the opening ceremony.

When she was finished, Senator Huffington frowned, his attention jumping from Susannah to

Hank Zarvy. "I thought you said the Alamo Rangers weren't prepared for the scope of this event."

"They aren't."

"It appears that they are, Mr. Zarvy."

"We can't afford to take chances, Senator."

"What we can't afford to do is step on the toes of my constituents. The Alamo is an historic landmark. Moving in a security team may look like a military takeover to the people of this community."

"It's the job of the planning committee to ensure that the Alamo is cared for and preserved for future generations. An extra security team is part of that."

"I don't think so." Senator Huffington stood. "And I'm not going to be part of it."

"But—" Zarvy was nearly purple with rage, but Huffington seemed unfazed.

"I said, I'm not going to be part of this, Zarvy. You can count out my security team. They'll report for duty on the sixth as indicated in Ms. Jorgenson's plans. Now, if you'll excuse me, I have another engagement." He walked out the door, and Zarvy speared Susannah with a look so filled with venom she took a step back.

"If anything happens at the opening ceremony, Ms. Jorgenson, I will hold you personally responsible." He stood, nearly knocking his chair over as he left the room. There was a murmur of voices, a rumble of sound as the room emptied.

"You were incredible, Susannah! I knew you were the right person for this job." Chad beamed from ear to ear as he patted her back.

"Thanks."

"Wish I could give you the day off, but I'll need you back at the Alamo tonight."

"No problem."

"Good. I'm working shift with you. See you then." He hurried out of the room, obviously jubilant.

Susannah wanted to feel the same, but all she felt was sick.

If anything happens at the opening ceremony, Ms. Jorgenson, I will hold you personally responsible.

"Smile, kid. You won." Oliver grinned, and Susannah tried to smile.

"It doesn't feel like a win. It feels like I just stapled a bull's-eye to my back."

"What you did was impress a lot of people. Including me." The sincerity in Levi's words was matched by the warmth in his eyes, and Susannah's cheeks heated.

"I agree." Melora Hudson moved toward them. "It was a well-thought-out presentation. I can see how much love you have for the site you're guarding."

"Thank you."

"Enjoy your day, and don't let Hank Zarvy's words worry you. He's all talk and very little action." She walked away, and Susannah took a deep breath.

"I guess that's it then."

"What's it?" Levi pressed a hand to her lower back, guiding her out of the room and onto the elevator.

"The Alamo Rangers keep control of the Alamo. And if anything goes wrong—"

"Nothing will."

"You can't know that, Levi." Anything could happen. All the preparation, all the training, all the foresight and planning, couldn't keep trouble from coming.

Susannah was living proof of that.

"No. I guess I can't, but I trust that it'll be true. I have faith that all those plans you put together will work out."

"More faith than me, I guess."

"Because I have more faith in you than you have in yourself."

It was true.

She knew it was.

She'd doubted herself for months. Doubted her ability to know good from bad, to know evil from righteousness. She'd thought Aaron was one person, and he'd been someone else entirely, and that had shaken her.

"I guess it's good someone has faith in me, because if something goes wrong, Zarvy will be gunning for me."

"Zarvy is a blowhard with more money than sense. You know that, right?" He shoved his hands into the pockets of his slacks, walking back toward the Alamo with long, brisk strides.

"Then why are you upset?"

"Who says I'm upset?"

"You're walking faster than I can ever hope to go."

"Sorry." He slowed, offered a half smile.

"What's wrong?"

"I don't like the idea of you continuing to work at the Alamo, and the more I think about it, the more I don't like it."

"I don't have a choice."

"Sure you do. Call Chad and tell him you can't be there."

"I don't work that way, Levi. I don't quit before I finish a job."

"I'm not saying you should quit. I'm saying you should play it safe."

"I played it safe when Aaron was stalking me. I got an alarm system. I watched my back. It didn't matter. What was going to happen, happened. The same is going to be true at the Alamo. We can put every security measure into place, but whatever is going to play out, will."

"Look, maybe I should just be blunt."

"Maybe you should."

"Work all you want all week, but today, I want you to go home, turn on your alarm and lock yourself in."

"Why?"

"I'm working rotation at the hospital tonight."

"The hospital?"

"We're keeping tabs on our key witness in Greg Pike's murder case. We need twenty-four-hour watch to make sure whoever tried to kill him doesn't make another attempt. Tonight is my shift."

"Okay."

"No. It's not okay. I can't be in two places at once, Susannah, and I don't want you at the Alamo alone."

"I'm not going to be alone. Chad will be there."

"Chad doesn't have a vested interest in your well-being."

"I'm not sure if I should be flattered by that comment or insulted."

"Neither. It's simply a statement of the facts as I see them." He stopped near her car, his hand resting on the hood of the Mustang.

"I'm a twenty-eight-year-old woman, Levi, perfectly capable of taking a vested interest in myself. I don't need you or Chad to take care of me. If anything else were the case, I wouldn't be able to do my job."

"Who said anything about anyone needing to take care of you?"

"It isn't what you said. It's what you didn't say." She opened the car door, dropped onto the seat.

Levi towered over her, but she didn't care. She was too frustrated and too tired to do more than glare at him.

He looked like he was going to argue.

Instead, he took a deep breath, shook his head. "You're right. There's plenty I didn't say. Like, even though we just recently reconnected I can't imagine life without you. Like, when I'm with you, I feel complete."

"Levi—"

"*That's* what I didn't say. And now you know why I don't want you working tonight. Now you understand why I want to be around to protect you."

"You don't have to—"

He leaned down, cutting off her words with a kiss that filled her up, emptied her out. All her thoughts gone. All her arguments spent.

And then he was backing up, moving away.

"I don't want you to work, but I understand why you have to. So, be careful, Susannah."

"I will." She agreed, not even sure she knew what he'd said. Her lips were still warm from his kiss, her pulse humming as he walked away.

A minute passed.

Then another.

Levi's scent still hovering around her, his kiss still warming her lips, but her mind was working again, telling her what she should have realized before: she'd just been distracted by a kiss.

She'd planned to remind Levi that she didn't need him or anyone else looking out for her.

One kiss and she'd forgotten everything she wanted to say, forgotten everything but how good it felt to be in his arms.

"Scoundrel," she muttered, pulling out onto Alamo Street.

But he was a charming one, a caring one.

So maybe not a scoundrel at all.

Maybe a guy she'd have loved once upon a time.

The thought was a bittersweet reminder of all she'd lost, and she pushed it away as she pulled up into her driveway and hurried into her empty house.

FIFTEEN

There was nothing more boring than guarding a silent witness. At least, not in Levi's opinion. He paced the small hospital room, wishing he could shake Quin awake and demand the guy open his mouth and speak. Once they got the information they needed from him, they could move him into protective custody in some other town, let the federal marshals take charge until the murder trial.

If there ever was a murder trial.

He shoved the doubts away, focusing his attention on the man who lay silent and still in the hospital bed. Quin had come close to dying, had been in a coma until recently, but for reasons Levi didn't understand, God had chosen to spare his life.

And take Gregory Pike's, instead.

All these months later, it still didn't make sense.

Quin stirred, shifting in his sleep and moaning softly. He was still too weak from his injuries to talk. It could be hours or days before he was finally able to speak, and there was no guarantee that what he would communicate would help put Pike's murderer in prison.

But the Texas Rangers of Company D were counting on Quin's memories. He was found shot and unconscious next to Gregory and was potentially the only witness to Greg's death. They were laying all their eggs in his basket and hoping it would pay off big-time. A name. A face. Surely Quin had seen something, knew something. They just had to keep him safe until he could speak, guard him until he was able to tell them what he knew.

Levi paced across the room again, stopping in front of the painting of the Alamo that decorated the wall. Quin had pointed to it more than once since he'd regained consciousness, gesturing with a deliberateness that left no doubt about his purpose. He was warning them. Whatever had gone down at Pike's house, it was connected to the Alamo.

And Susannah was there.

Levi didn't like it, had even thought about calling Chad and explaining all the reasons why it wasn't a good idea. Fortunately, his good sense prevailed and he'd let go of the idea, tried to let go of his worry. Susannah had survived a brutal attack, and she'd done it without a hero running to her rescue. She'd made it clear that she didn't need one now. He respected that.

But Levi wanted to be there for her. Reconnecting

with her had filled an empty place in his heart, a place he hadn't realized needed filling until Susannah stepped back into his life. He wasn't ready to let that go. He wasn't sure he ever would be.

Footsteps sounded outside the room, and Levi glanced at his watch. Nearly one in the morning. Could be the nurse was coming to check Quin's vitals. Could be a patient was wandering through the hospital.

Or it could be danger coming to call.

There'd already been one failed attempt on Quin's life, and Levi had no doubt that the men who were after him would try again if they had the opportunity. He didn't plan to give it to them. He moved to the door, waiting as the footsteps drew near. Voices carried into the room, a deeper voice and a higher-pitched one. A man and a woman. Nurse and patient? Man and wife?

A soft knock.

The doorknob turning.

Levi dropped a hand to the butt of his gun. Let it fall away as Captain Ben Fritz walked into the room, his fiancée, Greg Pike's daughter, Corinna, close to his side. They were dressed for an evening out. Ben in a sports coat, Corinna in a black dress that skimmed over her slim dancer's body.

"If bringing you to the hospital to visit a witness is Ben's idea of a good time, you might want to reconsider marrying him." He offered Corinna an easy smile, knowing that the last few months had been more than difficult for Greg's daughter. Losing her father had been bad enough, but knowing his killer was still free must be eating her up inside.

"I'd go anywhere with Ben. Even the hospital. Though I *can* think of a million other places I'd rather be." She returned his smile, but her gaze was on Quin, and she moved to the side of the bed, staring down at him as if she could will him to wake up and speak.

"So, what's up? Because I know for sure you wouldn't bring Corinna here if there wasn't something going on," Levi asked Ben.

"There's been more trouble at the Alamo."

"What kind of trouble?" Levi's pulse jumped, his mind going to a place he'd been trying to avoid all night.

Susannah, lying in a pool of blood, a knifeman standing above her.

"I don't have all the details. Just that they're transporting a patient here. I'm hoping she's coherent and able to give us a description, because this phantom intruder can *not* show up there Sunday."

"She?"

"One of the Alamo Rangers. I think—"

"When did you get the call?"

"Ten minutes ago."

"So they should be here by now."

"They were still stabilizing the patient when I left the theater."

Still stabilizing the patient?

"I'm going to need to ask you a huge favor, Ben."

"Ask? It looks like you've already decided I'm going to help out." Ben gestured toward the door Levi was opening.

"Can you call someone else in to babysit Quin?"

"I'm not sure anyone is going to be thrilled to hear from me this time of the night, but I'll give it a try. I take it you're going down to interview the patient."

Interview? That hadn't even occurred to him.

He went with it anyway.

"Right."

"I'll meet you once I find someone to fill in for you and get someone to escort Corinna home."

"There's no need for an escort. I can find my own way home." Corinna slid an arm around Ben's waist, and the look the two exchanged was so filled with secret messages and unspoken words that Levi had to look away.

"You can, but I'd rather you didn't."

"Ben—"

"I'm going to leave you to your argument. Corinna, it was nice seeing you again." Levi offered a quick wave and walked out of the room.

Soft sounds drifted into the corridor as he made his way through the unit. Beeps and hisses as machines breathed life into people. A cough. The sound of someone crying. That, more than any of the others, tore at Levi's heart. As much as hospitals were a place of healing, they were also a place of sorrow.

A nurse looked up as he approached the station, a soft smile hovering at the corners of her mouth. "Can I help you with something, Ranger?"

"A friend of mine is being transported here from the Alamo. I'd like to know where to meet the ambulance."

"I heard there was a patient coming in. I think their ETA is five minutes. Just go down to the first floor and follow the signs to Emergency. Someone there will be able to tell you more."

"Thanks."

"Don't mention it." She smiled again, went back to her paperwork, and Levi hurried onto the elevator, slamming his finger into the button and praying the door would close quickly.

It slid shut inch by agonizing inch, the elevator finally jerking to life. He wanted to claw the door open as soon as it reached the first floor, race through the lobby and into the emergency room.

"Can I help you, sir?" A young woman looked up from her place behind glass, a pleasant smile easing the tired lines of her face.

"A friend of mine is being brought here from the Alamo. I'd like to know if she's arrived yet."

"Name?"

"Susannah Jorgenson."

"Hold on." She typed the information into the computer and frowned. "She's not here yet. Let me check something else." She punched a few more keys, nodded. "Okay. We've got a transport coming from the Alamo. Two by ambulance. Looks like Trauma One." She frowned, the sympathy in her eyes settling deep in Levi's gut.

"Any idea what happened?"

"I can't say, sir, but you can go wait by the ambulance entrance if you'd like. That way you'll know when your friend arrives."

"Where's the ambulance going to unload?"

"Come on, and I'll show you." She opened a door, gestured for him to walk back through a long corridor lined with curtained triage areas. "See those double-wide doors? They'll come through there. Stay out of the way, though, and if anyone asks, I'm not the one who told you to wait there."

"Thanks," he offered, but his attention was already on the door and the sirens he could hear beyond it. Coming closer. Voices shouting. The door flying open.

He moved back, hugging the wall as an ambulance crew rolled a gurney in. Blankets covered the prone figure they were transporting, and Levi strained to see a face, hair, anything.

"Sir, you're going to have to go back to the

waiting room." A dark-haired man approached, his gaze dropping from Levi's face to his badge and then settling on his face again. "The patient is in no shape to answer your questions."

"I'm not here to ask questions. I'm here to make sure she's okay."

"Levi?"

He turned as a second gurney was pushed toward him, Susannah levered up on her elbows on top of it, her emerald eyes staring out from a stark white face.

"Ma'am, you need to lie back." An EMT pressed her back down as Levi ran to her side, tried to assess the damage. Her shirt had been ripped from her shoulder and thick gauze pads soaked up blood. Too much blood.

"What happened?"

"I thought you weren't here to question me." She offered a weak smile, reaching for his hand and holding on tight.

"I'm not." But he wanted to, because he wanted to find the person who'd hurt her and make him pay. Anger clawed at his gut, made him want to storm from the hospital and track down the criminals. Made him want to forget that he was a Texas Ranger, sworn to uphold the law, and not a vigilante.

"You are." She squeezed his hand, but her grip weakened, her fingers barely clasping his. He tightened his hold, refusing to let go as she was wheeled into triage.

"Sir, you're going to have to leave." A security guard approached, saw Levi's badge and paused. "Sorry, Ranger, but I've been asked to get you out of here. They need to work on your friend."

Levi nodded, but he didn't want to leave, didn't want to let go.

"Are you going to be okay?" He leaned close, whispering in Susannah's ear.

"Yes, but I need you to do something for me."

"What's that?"

"Find out about Chad. He…didn't look good when I found him."

"Found him?"

"We were doing rounds. He was on the east side. I was in the gardens. He called for help, and I ran, but I got there too late. He'd already been shot. Next thing I knew, I was hit." She blinked rapidly, and he knew she was trying to hold back tears.

"It's okay, Susannah."

"No. It's not. He has a family, Levi. Kids and a wife. Go make sure he's okay. Please. I have to know."

He nodded, pressing a kiss to her forehead before backing away.

It hurt more than he'd thought it could. Hurt to the depth of his soul to walk away from her. He'd watched her grow up. Little Susannah with the wild red curls turning into an awkward adolescent, then a graceful teen. He hadn't realized how much he'd missed her until he saw her again, but if she disappeared from his life, he didn't think the missing would ever stop.

"Hey, Levi! What's going on? I got a call from Ben. He said there's been more trouble. Said a couple of Alamo Rangers had been shot." Oliver hurried across the emergency room waiting area.

"That's all the information I have. Susannah—"

"Susannah was shot?"

"Yes. She and Chad were doing rounds. Chad must have run into someone on the grounds. He called for help, and Susannah found him shot. She was going toward him when she was shot."

"She should have secured the area first." Oliver shoved change into a vending machine, his comment making Levi want to wring his neck.

"If you'd been the one bleeding to death, would you be saying the same?"

"Don't know." Oliver shoved a handful of peanuts into his mouth. "I just know what she should have done. Find the perp. Make sure he's disarmed. Then tend to the wounded."

"Right. I need to go see if there's news on Chad."

"They'll come out and tell us if he makes it."

Levi ignored the comment and ignored the urge to slam his fist into Oliver's peanut-filled mouth. The receptionist who'd let him into the treatment area looked up as he approached. “Sorry. I can’t let you back there again. My supervisor wasn’t happy.”

“I’m just trying to find out if the patient transported from the Alamo is doing okay.”

“The man or woman?”

“Man.”

“He’s holding his own. Doc says the bullet missed the guy’s heart by a quarter of an inch. He’s already in surgery, but it looks like he’s going to pull through fine. I’ll let you know when he’s moved to the intensive care unit. I doubt you’ll be able to visit until tomorrow.”

“How about Susannah? Is she in surgery?”

“Let me check.” She typed something into the computer. “Looks like there’s good news there, too. No surgery scheduled. Must mean things weren’t as serious as they’d thought.”

Or as serious as they’d looked.

“Thanks.”

“No problem. I’ll let you know if anything changes.”

Levi nodded, pacing back across the room and ignoring Oliver’s curious stare. “I need to call the Alamo. See who’s in charge there and find out what’s going on.”

“Already done. Ben sent Daniel Riley to keep an eye on things.”

“And?”

"There are a couple dozen San Antonio police officers scouring the grounds. So far, all they've found is a bullet casing and set of keys to the Alamo. They're not sure if they belonged to one of our victims or to our perp. I'm hoping for the perp. If he's lost his means of entry, we'll have a lot more luck keeping him out of the compound."

"Isn't that like locking the door to the coop after the fox has already eaten the chickens? We've got two Rangers down. Finding the perp's keys isn't going to change that," Levi muttered, pulling out his phone, but not sure who to call. What he wanted to do was leave the hospital, go to the Alamo, help with the investigation.

More than that, he wanted to find Susannah again and make sure she really was okay.

"Hey, as sorry as I am about what happened, if it means the site is secure for Sunday's ceremony, it's to our advantage."

"You're a cold son of a gun, Drew." Something he hadn't realized about his fellow Company D member until that moment.

"Not cold. Practical. If anything happens on our watch, we'll lose our jobs. I'm not sure about you, but I can't afford to let that happen."

"I'm going to find Susannah." Levi turned away, afraid of what he'd say if he stuck around Oliver for too long. Though they were both members of

Company D, they'd never been more than acquaintances. Levi was beginning to understand why.

He crossed the room, bypassing the receptionist and opening the door to the triage area. She watched him walk through but didn't comment. It was for the best. He wasn't going to stop. Not for her. Not for the security guard. Not until he'd found Susannah, and not until he'd found the person who'd shot her.

SIXTEEN

Susannah crossed the hospital room on wobbly legs, dragging the IV pole along with her. The bandages on her shoulder were thick and bulky, the deep ache from the gunshot wound throbbing intensely. She pulled the door open and stepped into the hall.

"Making your escape?" Levi's deep voice rumbled behind her, and she turned, her foot catching on the bottom of the pole, her legs going out from under her.

"Whoa! Careful." His hands settled on her waist, supporting her as she caught her balance and her breath.

"Thanks." She gritted her teeth, wishing she'd taken the nurse up on the offer of pain medicine. Of course, if she had, she'd be closing in on unconsciousness, and there was no way she wanted that. She needed to make sure Chad was okay, and then she needed to get back to the Alamo.

"No problem." His fingers were warm through her hospital gown, his muscles taut and hard.

"Have you heard anything about Chad?" She didn't bother with niceties, didn't have the energy or the time for them.

"He's in surgery. It looks like he's going to make it."

"Thank you, Lord," she whispered, and Levi nodded.

"God was definitely looking out for him."

"I need to call his family and let them know what's happened."

"San Antonio P.D. will take care of informing the family. You need to get into bed and rest." He tried to steer her back to the room, but Susannah wasn't going. She'd had enough of hospitals after Aaron's attack; nearly two weeks in the intensive care, another two weeks easing off pain medicine and IVs and back onto regular food.

"I'm going back to the Alamo." But her feet wouldn't move, her leaden body refused to cooperate.

"And do what?"

Good question. No doubt there were dozens of officers and Rangers scouring the grounds. They didn't need her help, and in her weakened condition she'd probably only be in the way.

"See if I can figure out what happened." Because she really didn't know. She and Chad were heading out on rounds. Gates were closed, compound quiet, everything just as it should be. Until it wasn't.

"That can wait for another day." He slipped an arm around her waist, started leading her back to the room.

"The first twenty-four hours are the most important in any case. You know that, Levi."

"And I know the investigation is being conducted. Leads are already being followed. You resting won't keep any of those things from happening."

"If you were capable of getting up and going, would you lie in bed while someone else investigated a case for you?"

"No, but I'm a trained law officer. It's my job to investigate crimes and seek criminals. As long as I have it in me to do it, I will."

"Then you'll understand why I feel the way I do. I signed up to keep the Alamo secure. I failed. I need to go see what kind of damage has been done."

"No damage, but they found keys and a bullet casing."

"Keys?"

"My understanding is that it was an entire set. The responding officers weren't sure if they were yours or Chad's or if the perp dropped them."

"Mine were hanging from my belt. They were still there when the ambulance came. I'm not sure about Chad's."

"I'll see if I can find out." He urged her back into the room, and she almost considered climbing into bed and letting Levi and the rest of the team secure the Alamo and investigate the shooting.

Almost.

But despite the throbbing pain in her shoulder, she felt hyped up and ready for action. "Can you find a nurse while you're at it? I want to get this IV out and get out of here."

He frowned, and she was sure he'd refuse.

"For the record, I think this is a bad idea."

"For the record, I appreciate the fact that you're not trying to keep me from making my own decision about it."

He smiled, tugging at one of her curls before he walked out of the room.

She grabbed what was left of her uniform from the chair next to the bed, pulling on the slacks and frowning at the shirt. The EMTs had cut away the top when they'd arrived, and there was little left but ribbons of fabric.

"Ms. Jorgenson?" A soft knock followed the query, and the door opened, a tall, spare woman walking in. "I'm Dr. Williamson. I hear you want to leave."

"I'll rest better at home."

"Maybe so, but I can't recommend that you go any earlier than tomorrow night. Mind if I take a look at the wound?" She gestured to the bed, and

Susannah sat on the edge of it while the doctor examined the stitched gash in the fleshy part of her shoulder.

"Looks like it's dry. No more bleeding. Not bad. You should heal up in a couple of weeks. A lot better than your buddy, but it looks like even he's going to make it. I guess you were both fortunate tonight." She offered a brief smile.

"You treated Chad?" Susannah asked as she pulled her hospital gown back into place.

"I assisted during the surgery. A half inch either way and he'd be dead."

"I'd like to see him."

"You'll have to wait a couple days. We're keeping him in a medically induced coma for at least forty-eight hours and letting the ventilator work for him. Until he's stable, only family can visit."

It sounded bad. Really bad. But when Susannah had found him lying in a pool of his own blood, felt his thready pulse beneath her fingers, she'd thought he would die before the ambulance arrived, had prayed desperately while she applied pressure to the spurting wound.

Yeah, an induced coma was bad, but being dead was worse, and she silently thanked God again for sparing Chad's life.

"Everything okay in here?" Levi walked into the room.

"Fine."

"Except that we're not in agreement over where you're going to spend the night." Dr. Williamson jotted something on Susannah's chart, offering Levi a cursory glance.

"Like I said, I'll be more comfortable at home."

"If you're insistent, I'll have the nurse take out your IV, but I'd really rather you stay."

"I'm going to have to insist, then."

"I'll write out a prescription for pain medication, but if you experience any dizziness, lose consciousness or have shortness of breath, you need to come back in immediately."

"I will."

"All right. The nurse should be in momentarily." The doctor frowned, wrote something else on the chart and left the room.

"If you're taking a vote, I'll weigh in on the side of the doctor." Levi dropped onto the bed, his eyes deeply shadowed, his hair ruffled as if he'd run his fingers through it again and again.

"Are you okay?" She touched his knuckles, heat shooting up her arm at the contact, her heart leaping as he looked into her eyes.

"Seeing as how I didn't just get shot, I'd say I'm doing pretty well." He turned his hand over and captured hers, his callused palm rough and cool against her heated skin.

"You look tired."

"It's been a long couple of days."

"Once we get through Sunday, things should calm down," she responded without thinking, her body sagging toward his of its own accord until their shoulders touched, their arms pressed together.

"I don't think you're going to be up to security detail Sunday." He pressed her head to his shoulder, his palm resting against her neck, his thumb skimming back and forth along her jaw.

"I'll be up to it." Though right at that moment, she thought she'd be content to sit right where she was forever.

"Susie, I want you to stay away from the Alamo until after the ceremony." His words seeped through her contented haze, and Susannah straightened.

"I thought we agreed that I make my own decisions."

"You could have been killed tonight."

"I could have been killed last summer, too, but I wasn't." She stood, her legs shaky.

"Sus—"

"I have to keep going, Levi. If I don't, I'll climb into bed, pull the covers over my head and stay there forever. That's how bad the fear is. How real it is. So, please, stop tempting me to hide away until all this blows over. We might find our perp, we might throw him in jail, we might even get through the ceremony without any trouble, but what's inside of me isn't going to blow over. It's always going to be there, and I'm always going to be fighting it." Her throat burned as the words poured out, and she turned away, blinking back hot tears.

She shouldn't have said that.

Didn't know why she had.

"I'm sorry."

"Why? It's not your fault. It's just…who I am."

"Whatever you need to do, Susannah, I'll stand beside you." The sincerity in his voice pierced her heart, and the tears she didn't want to shed slid down her cheeks. She brushed them away, impatient and irritated and sad. Sad because she wasn't who she wanted to be. A woman who could look in Levi's eyes, see the interest and attraction there and throw herself heart first into it.

"It's going to be okay." He pulled her into his arms, and she went willingly, let her head rest against his chest. His heart thumped beneath her ear, the steady easy rhythm of it seeping into her, tempting her to believe that he was right. That everything really would be okay.

"Ms. Jorgenson?"

Susannah jumped, whirling to face a smiling nurse. "Yes?"

"Dr. Williamson sent me to remove your IV. It will only take a minute."

"Thanks." She sat, offering her arm and turning away.

Just another minute and she and Levi could be

on their way back to the Alamo where an intruder had lain in wait.

She shuddered, and the nurse frowned as she pressed gauze and a bandage to the inside of Susannah's elbow. "You look very pale."

"I'm fine."

"You're shaking." The nurse frowned again, pressing a cool hand against Susannah's forehead. "I think I'd better call Dr.—"

"She just needs a little fresh air," Levi cut in. Not because he wanted Susannah to leave the hospital. She knew that, knew that if he could have convinced her to stay, he'd have done so.

No. He didn't want her to leave, but he'd support her choice, give her whatever help he could.

That meant a lot.

Probably more than he knew.

"I think you're making a mistake, but we can't force you to stay. Here are the doctor's instructions and a prescription for pain meds. I'll go get a wheelchair."

"Don't bother. I can—"

"She'll have to argue if you decline the ride, so you may as well let her go." Levi pulled Susannah to her feet as the nurse left the room.

"I'm not in the mood to wait."

"I said she'd argue. I didn't say you had to wait." He cupped her elbow, offering subtle support as they walked out into the corridor.

"Still a rule-breaker like you were when you were a kid?"

"Only when it's necessary."

"I'm glad. The hospital was getting to me. The smells and sounds and..."

"Memories?"

"Those, too." They stepped into the elevator, and Susannah pushed the button for the ground floor. "I wonder which floor the ICU is on?"

"First."

"Maybe—"

"It's not going to happen."

"You don't even know what I was going to say."

"Sure I do. You were going to say that we could stop by the ICU and visit Chad, but I already tried and security turned me away."

"The doctor said he's on a ventilator."

"I know."

"He should be home with his wife and kids, getting ready for another day to begin. Not lying in a hospital bed fighting for his life." She swallowed back tears. She'd shed enough for one day.

"At least he has his life to fight for. Thanks to you."

"It doesn't feel that way. It feels like I failed him."

"I understand."

"Do you?"

"Every day that we don't find Greg's killer is another day that I feel I've failed him."

They stepped off the elevator, and Susannah looked into Levi's eyes. Really looked. She'd heard the news reports. She knew that the Rangers of Company D had arrived at Gregory Pike's house and found him dead, but knowing it was different than seeing it in Levi's eyes. Feeling his helplessness, his rage, his grief.

"There was nothing you could do, Levi. You know that, right?"

"Head knowledge can't always change the heart, and my heart says I failed."

"I don't think Captain Pike would agree."

"Too bad he's not around to ask." He offered a half smile as they stepped outside.

"If he were—"

"You'd better wear this. It's chilly and hospital gowns don't offer much protection." He shrugged out of his jacket, tucked it around her shoulders, his hands gentle, his touch so light she barely felt it.

"Changing the subject?"

"And making sure you stay warm. I guess you could call that killing two birds with one stone."

He had a right to his silence, a right to his secrets. Susannah had enough of her own to know that she should respect the boundaries he'd set, not push for more information than he wanted to give.

She *wanted* to push, though, wanted to ask and learn and understand.

And that scared her.

Asking, learning, understanding, those were the building blocks of trust. Trust was the foundation of a relationship. A relationship…

A relationship was something she'd once longed for, but had given up believing in. She was too damaged, too scarred, and she didn't want to put that on someone else.

But maybe she could.

Maybe that's what this was about. Her being with Levi. Him being with her. The two of them working together toward a common goal. They both needed to heal. They both needed to move on. Maybe God planned for them to do that together.

Levi opened his car door, and Susannah dropped into the seat, her shoulder throbbing with the movement. Compared to what she'd felt after Aaron's attack, the pain was merely an annoyance. She leaned her head back, closing her eyes, Levi's jacket warming her, his scent filling her, settling deep into her mind as he pulled out of the parking lot and headed toward the Alamo.

SEVENTEEN

He should take her home.

Levi knew it, but he didn't have the heart to drive Susannah back to her place.

"You're quiet," she said, and he cast a quick look in her direction.

Her eyes were closed, curly hair framing her face.

"Just thinking that I'm making a mistake."

"By taking me to the Alamo?"

"It's a crime scene, and you're a civilian." And he was allowing his heart to lead his head. Not good when he had a job to focus on.

"I'm also a security guard there. Not to mention a witness to the crime."

"A wounded one."

"It barely hurts."

"Then why are your eyes closed?"

"Because I'm trying to remember what happened, trying to bring it into my mind as clear and crisp as I can get it. The more I remember, the easier it will be for your people to track down the guy responsible."

"San Antonio P.D. is running the investigation." But the Rangers would be involved. They had a vested interest in the Alamo, and until they knew why Quin kept gesturing to the picture of it, they'd keep their fingers on its pulse. What they couldn't do was step on toes, get in the way, offer support that SAPD didn't need.

"But your people will be there, too."

"True."

"And I'm sure some of my coworkers will be there. So, I'll fit right in."

"I hate to break the news to you, Susie, but walking around in a hospital gown isn't going to make you fit in anywhere except a hospital."

"I'll borrow a shirt from someone." She sounded so completely unperturbed that Levi laughed.

"What?" She straightened, and he felt her gaze without looking at her. It was a physical touch, drifting from his cheek to his neck to his hands.

"You have three inches of gauze on your shoulder, you're pale as a ghost, and you look more like a seventeen-year-old kid than a security professional. There is no way you won't be noticed if you go wandering around the crime scene."

"I'm not planning to wander. I'm planning to listen."

"To?"

"Everyone. Everything. The guy who shot me he wasn't a stranger."

"You saw him?" Levi's pulse leaped at the idea his mind racing with a hundred possibilities.

"He was standing in the shadows while I was trying to stop Chad from bleeding to death. I didn't see him at first. By the time I did, it was too late."

"You recognized him, though?"

"I had the sense that I knew him. That something about the way he stood and moved was very familiar. I keep thinking he's Aaron, but he's not. That only leaves one other option—he's someone else I know."

"Fear can play funny tricks on our minds."

"True, but I don't think that's what happened tonight."

"I'm not saying you didn't see someone you know."

"You don't have to. I've been trying to convince myself that I was mistaken for the past hour. I can't. Whoever is doing this is someone I know. I'm hoping he's going to be at the Alamo tonight and I'm hoping that if he is, I'll recognize him."

"That's a dangerous game, Susannah."

"No more dangerous than hiding away and hoping he won't come after me again."

"You're assuming he was after you. He shot Chad first. You may have just been in the way."

"Who he was after doesn't matter. You said it

before, Levi, and I didn't want to believe it. Someone on the Alamo Rangers' team is behind this. It's the only explanation that makes sense."

She was right.

But there were more than two dozen Rangers. Fourteen were men, each one innocent until proven guilty. So far, four had been in for polygraph tests. All four had passed. Ten more to go, and Levi was confident one of them was on the Lions' payroll.

"Okay. So, you're coming with me. You're staying out of the way, and you're keeping your eyes and your ears open."

"Sounds like a plan." There was a smile in her voice, and she patted his knee as if all the years between them didn't exist.

Maybe they didn't.

Or maybe they simply didn't matter anymore.

His phone rang, and he grabbed it, holding it to his ear as he pulled up behind a police cruiser parked in front of the Alamo. The entrance to the building was blocked by an evidence van, and several officers were standing guard.

"Hello?"

"Levi. It's Ben."

"What's up?"

"Are you on your way to the Alamo?"

"I just pulled up in front of it."

"Good. San Antonio P.D. just called. Said there

was something there they wanted us to see. Apparently, the gunman left a calling card."

"A rose?"

"A couple dozen."

"Anything else?" He glanced at Susannah. She was staring out the window, her attention on the Alamo, but he knew she was listening to every word.

"A photograph of an Alamo Ranger getting in a car. She's pretty. Early twenties."

"Late twenties, but who's counting," Susannah muttered, pushing open the door and letting cool air rush in.

"We'll take a look."

"Is Oliver with you?"

"No. He's still at the hospital, waiting for more news on the male gunshot victim."

"That's Chad Morran, right?"

"Yes."

"And the other victim?"

"Susannah."

"You suspected as much."

"But I hoped I was wrong."

"Is she still at the hospital?"

"No. She's with me."

"You're at the Alamo."

"Right."

"You've brought a victim back to the scene?"

"Yes."

"Not a good idea, McDonall."

"Too late. We're already here. I'll check back in after I see what San Antonio P.D. has collected." He hung up before Ben could offer a hundred reasons why having Susannah with him wasn't a good idea.

"If you're going to get into trouble for bringing me here, I'll go home." Susannah spoke quietly, giving Levi an out he should have jumped at, but didn't.

"A little trouble never hurt anyone. Come on. Let's see what those roses look like."

"I already know what they look like. Long-stemmed. Red. No thorns."

"He had to get them from somewhere. Maybe we can trace him that way."

"There are hundreds of florists around here. It'll take a week to contact all of them."

"That's not defeat I hear, is it?" He tugged her out of the car, slipping an arm around her waist as they moved toward the Alamo.

"I don't know the meaning of the word." But she sounded tired, and he thought about turning around, helping her back into the car and driving her home.

"I'm afraid you can't come any closer." A police officer stopped them a hundred yards from the chapel entrance, and Levi introduced himself, flashed his badge and waited while the officer checked his credentials.

"You're clear to go through, but your friend will have to stay."

"She was one of the victims. I want to have her look at the crime scene, see if it jogs any memories."

"Good to see you up and moving around, ma'am." The officer moved aside, calling the information in on his radio while Levi and Susannah walked into the chapel.

Another officer met them there. He greeted Levi with a firm handshake. "Sergeant Jason Richardson."

"Ranger Levi McDonall. This is Susannah Jorgenson."

"Ma'am. Sorry we're meeting under such terrible circumstances, but I'm glad to see your injuries weren't life-threatening. I heard the other vict… Your coworker is going to make it."

"It looks that way."

"Good. I planned on coming to the hospital to interview you, but if you're up to it, I can do that now."

"That's why I'm here, Sergeant."

"Great." He asked her several questions as they walked through the chapel and out into the compound, and Levi only half listened to the answers. Whatever had gone down, it hadn't been planned.

The more he thought about it, the more sure he was about that. The fact that more roses had been discovered on the compound only seemed to confirm his theory. The intruder had meant to drop the roses and leave, but Chad had gotten in the way.

"All right. Thank you for cooperating, Ms. Jorgenson. I know this has been a stressful night. I just have one more thing I'd like you to do for me. We found something on the ground behind the long barracks. More than one thing, actually. You up to taking a look?"

"Sure." But her voice was weak.

"You don't have to do this, Susannah."

"Yes, I do," she said, but she didn't resist when Levi pulled her to his side, offered support as they walked to the long barracks.

Several teams worked the ground beside the building, crisscrossing the path and the grassy area beyond it. A dozen feet away, a man snapped photos of the pavement, capturing a dark stain that glistened in the flash from the camera.

"That's a lot of blood," Susannah said quietly, and Levi squeezed her hand.

"Our perp wasn't playing around, that's for sure," the sergeant responded, leading them past the wide stain and around the building. A woman stood in the shadows there, snapping photos of a pile of roses that lay abandoned on the ground.

She frowned as they approached, stepping back, but continuing with her job.

"So, here's what we found." Richardson crouched close to the bouquets. "Ring any bells?"

"Yes." Susannah offered a quick explanation as she studied the roses.

"And how about this?" Richardson used a gloved hand to lift a Polaroid picture, and Susannah nodded.

"I've never seen the photo, but that's me coming out of my house. It looks like it was taken recently."

"Not very likely you have another stalker." Richardson rubbed the back of his neck, scanning the area as if he could find more clues hidden there.

"No."

"Someone is going through a lot of trouble to make you think you do. Why would that be?"

"She's lead security officer for the opening ceremony at the Alamo this weekend. We think the perp was trying to scare her into leaving."

"To what end?"

"To further the cause of a group called the Lions of Texas."

"I just recently started hearing about them. There was a big sting down near the border, right? A sheriff and a border patrol agent taken into custody."

"That's right. We believe Captain Gregory Pike

was investigating the Lions when he was killed. We also believe the Lions are planning something for the day of the opening ceremony."

"Not something good, I take it."

"No."

Richardson whistled softly and shook his head. "Big troubles around these parts, for sure."

"What's going on here?" Hank Zarvy stepped around the side of the barracks and speared Levi with a look designed to make him cower.

Too bad he wasn't a cowering kind of guy.

"This is a crime scene, Mr. Zarvy. It's probably best if you wait outside the compound. We'll fill you in on the details of our investigation when we finish here." Richardson seemed as unimpressed by Zarvy's show of force as Levi was.

"Crime scene? This is a historical landmark. One that is going to be hosting the governor, the lieutenant governor and the vice president of the United States in just a few days. Your men are tromping all over the grounds like a bunch of first graders at the playground."

"We're doing our job and making sure we do it thoroughly."

"If you were doing it thoroughly you'd have someone in jail already," Zarvy snapped, his attention on Susannah. "You're the woman who insisted things were under control, right? The one who had a foolproof security plan in place."

"I never said it was foolproof."

"You implied it. Now look what we've got. The compound is trashed, the press is camping outside." He slashed his hand through the air. "It's a mess. We'll be lucky if our guest speakers don't cancel on us."

"We're celebrating the 175th anniversary of the Battle of the Alamo, but we're also celebrating the resiliency and determination of Texas and of her people. I'm sure that the trouble we're having will rally rather than scare our guest speakers." Susannah's words seemed to take some of the wind out of Zarvy's sail. His arm dropped to his side, and he rubbed the bridge of his nose.

"We have got to get this place under control before Sunday. Do you understand that, Ms. Jorgenson?"

"Of course."

"Then do it, because if you don't, *I* will, and that will mean you and a lot of your coworkers will be finding other jobs." He stalked off without another sound, and Susannah sagged, leaning her back against the wall of the barracks as if she could barely hold herself up.

"Well, that was fun." Her smile was brittle, and Levi wanted to pull her into his arms, let her rest against his chest.

"That guy never ceases to amaze me. I'd rather walk through a pit filled with a hundred rattlers

than deal with him. Come on. I'll walk you out."
Richardson led the way back to the chapel, leaving them with a curt reminder to call if anything came up.

"I guess there's nothing more I can do here. Would you mind giving me a ride home? I don't think I can drive." Susannah looked ready to collapse, her face parchment-pale, her eyes emerald fire against pallid skin.

"I don't think I could let you drive even if you wanted to." He thought she'd rise to the bait and tell him it wasn't his decision, but she simply shrugged.

"You'd get no argument from me. The adrenaline is gone, and so is my energy."

"It wouldn't be a bad thing to take the next few days off."

"I can't. I need to find out who did this, Levi. I need to know why." She got in the car, wincing as she settled into the seat.

"It's not your job to find out, Susannah, and digging too deep, looking too hard could get you into the kind of trouble you can't get out of."

"Then what do you suggest I do? Sit twiddling my thumbs while everyone else tries to solve my problems?"

"If it keeps you alive, yes." He shut the door, knowing she wasn't going to listen, and was more frustrated by that than he should be.

She wasn't a kid. She was a grown woman who carried a gun to work, a grown woman who'd proven again and again that she could take care of herself.

A grown woman he was falling in love with.

Falling?

He'd fallen.

"We need to call all the Alamo Rangers into work tomorrow. Maybe you can get all the polygraphs done in one day."

"The test has to be administered at our office. Hopefully we can get a few more done tomorrow. A few more the day after that."

"And have our man by the opening ceremony?"

"Exactly."

"Do you think he'll talk once you bring him in? Tell you who hired him and why?"

"I hope he will, but there's no guarantee. Even if he does, if he's an underling in the Lions' organization, he won't know much about what the upper tier is doing or who is operating it."

"Maybe I could spend time with each of the other Rangers. Try to figure out which one I saw tonight."

"Susannah." He pulled up in front of her house, turning to face her. "I know you want answers, but I meant what I said. Don't dig. Don't go looking. Let us handle things."

"I can't."

"You don't have a choice."

Her jaw tightened, anger flashing in her eyes, but she didn't argue, just got out of the car and walked to the porch. He followed, grabbing her hand and pulling her to a stop when she would have gone inside.

"I didn't say that to make you angry. I said it because it's the truth. This isn't about you or me, Susie. It's not about how we feel for one another. It's about closing down a drug cartel. It's about finding Gregory Pike's murderer. It's about keeping three very high-ranking politicians alive."

"I know."

"Then don't fight me when I say you need to stay home and rest."

"I..." She shook her head, bright light spilling onto her hair, splashing onto high cheekbones and the shadowy crescents beneath her eyes.

"What?"

"I've never known anyone else like you, Levi. I've never wanted so badly to be part of someone's life. His dreams. His hopes. Never."

"Is that a bad thing?"

"Only when it keeps me from doing what I feel I should."

"Does that mean you're going to stay out of the investigation?"

"It means I value your opinion about it."

"That's not an answer."

"It's all I have right now." She unlocked the door and stepped into the house, disarming the security system, her hand shaking as she pushed the buttons.

"Then it's enough. Come on. You're exhausted, wounded. Right now, what you need to do is heal." He led her to the sofa, urged her to lie down, then dragged an afghan from the back of a chair and covered her with it.

"Thank you." She grabbed his hand, held it to her cheek, her skin smooth and silky beneath his palm.

"Thank me by staying here and getting better." He crouched beside her, inhaling antiseptic, the coppery scent of blood and, beneath it all, the subtle flowery scent that was Susannah.

"I'm so tired, I don't think I have a choice."

"Good night, Susie." He brushed his lips against hers, his heart throbbing with such deep longing it took him by surprise.

She felt it, too. He could see it in her eyes, feel it in the rapid intake of her breath.

"Keep the alarm on. I'll see you tomorrow." He ran a finger along her cheek, felt the silkiness of her skin again, then forced himself to get up, walk outside and shut the door.

On Susannah.

On his own desperate need for her.

There would be time to explore their relationship, but now wasn't it.

Now was the time for finding the man who'd shot her and making sure he paid for it.

EIGHTEEN

"*See you tomorrow* must be man-speak for *you're on your own, kid*," Susannah muttered as she eased a silky shirt over thick bandages and buttoned it.

Six days since Levi had uttered those words, and she still hadn't seen him.

She'd talked to him.

Talked to him plenty.

He'd called every day, kept her updated on preparations for the opening ceremony, kept her abreast of new leads in the investigation into the shooting.

He'd done everything but come for a visit.

Which was fine.

Susannah had kept busy. Her personal physician might have forbidden her from returning to work but she'd kept in contact with her coworkers, made sure that the security plans she'd created were being implemented.

It wasn't easy taking a backseat after months of planning, but she'd done it, and now she was going to the Alamo. She might not be able to be part of the security team, but Jeremy Camp, who'd taken over as lead security officer, had promised she'd have access to the ceremony. She'd sit in the audience, relax and pray that things went off without a hitch.

She grabbed her purse, walked to the foyer.

Open the door.

Walk outside.

Enjoy the day.

It should have been easy.

It wasn't.

Aside from a trip to her doctor, she'd spent the past few days hunkered down and healing. Doctor's orders, and she'd followed them to a T. Had let them be her excuse, but they couldn't be her excuse forever.

She opened the door, her heart racing, her palms sweaty, everything inside screaming *danger.* But there was no danger, just gorgeous golden dawn and silvery blue sky and a truck parked across the street from her house. A man staring at her. Handsome face. Clean-shaven. Vaguely familiar, but she couldn't quite place him.

He opened the door, got out of the truck, calling to her when she would have gone back inside and slammed the door.

"Ms. Jorgenson?" He knew her name, but that

didn't mean he was a friend. She moved closer to the door, ready for a quick escape if she needed one.

"Yes."

"Lieutenant Daniel Riley. Texas Rangers, Company D. We met briefly a few days ago when you and Levi were chasing down a blue Mitsubishi." He pulled a wallet form the pocket of his suit jacket, let her take a long look at his ID.

"That's right. I remember. What can I do for you, Lieutenant Riley?"

"I'm here to escort you to the Alamo."

"That's not necessary."

"Levi thinks it is, and since he's caught up in security prep, he asked me to make sure you arrived safely."

"I appreciate the offer, but I'd rather drive there myself."

"I wouldn't call it an offer. Levi has threatened my very life and limb if I don't bring you directly to the Alamo. I'm afraid, Ms. Jorgenson, that's exactly what I'm going to have to do."

"Lieu—" Her cell phone rang, and Daniel motioned for her to answer it.

She did so quickly, never taking her eyes off Lieutenant Riley. He carried a badge and probably a gun, but that didn't make him one of the good guys. "Hello?"

"Are you giving my friend trouble?" Levi's voice was smooth as melted chocolate and twice as decadent.

"You shouldn't have sent him here."

"I would have come myself, but I needed to be on-site. There's a small memorial service planned for ten this morning. A way to honor Daniel's father, Robert Riley. It's very private and very quiet." Robert Riley had been a much-loved and vital part of the San Antonio community, and the Alamo anniversary celebration had been dedicated to him.

"I remember. The ceremony is immediately following the memorial."

"And since Daniel is attending both, I knew it wouldn't be a problem for him to stop and give you a ride."

"You still shouldn't have sent him here. I'm perfectly capable of driving myself."

"It's not about being capable. It's about being safe."

"I've been safe for six days. Why would anyth—"

"I hate to cut the argument short, but we need to get moving. The traffic is going to be bad, and I don't want to be late," Daniel cut in, looking more amused than rushed.

"I have to go, Levi."

"I'll see you when you get here."

"I'm not sure I'm going to—" But he'd already

disconnected, and Susannah tossed the phone into her bag, frowning as she pulled the front door closed and locked it.

"All set?" Daniel asked, and she nodded.

"I'm really sorry about this. I know you have more important things to do with your time."

"If I did, I wouldn't be here." He smiled as he helped her into the truck. "I'll be helping with security later. For now, I'm just going to sit and listen to people's memories of my father."

"You must miss him terribly."

"We weren't close, but that doesn't mean I can't appreciate what others have to say about him." He pulled out onto the road, navigating the seven miles to the Alamo quickly. Traffic had already backed up on Alamo Street, and Daniel eased into a restricted parking area, pulling his truck in next to a black Cadillac.

Banners decorated streetlights and potted flowers lined the path leading to the Alamo, and Susannah could feel the excitement of it thrumming through her veins, feel her heartbeat mixing with the cacophony of noise, the pulse of San Antonio.

Policemen formed human barricades, blocking the crowd that pressed in to watch the motorcade of VIPs. Daniel showed his ID, and Susannah followed him to the Alamo Chapel, inhaling the scent of age and history as she walked into the cool building.

It was quiet there, several dozen people sitting in rows of chairs that faced a podium.

"Daniel!" A slim, pretty woman ran toward them, throwing her arms around Susannah's escort and offering a kind smile. Melora Hudson. This time Susannah had no trouble recognizing the woman.

"Susannah, I'm so glad you're feeling better. I couldn't believe it when I heard you'd been shot! I was so inspired by your confident presentation to the Alamo Planning Committee, and I really hope we'll have you back working to secure the Alamo soon."

"The doctor thinks I'll be able to go back in a couple of weeks."

"Good. We need more people like you here. It's such a wonderful testimony to the history of our state and our people. It really does need to be protected."

"I agree."

"Agree with what?" Levi rumbled, and Susannah turned to face him, her breath catching in her throat, her heart skipping a beat. Dark slacks encased long, muscular legs. A white dress shirt hugged a perfectly carved chest. A navy tie. A Ranger's badge. Deep brown eyes that welcomed her to look again and again and again.

He was gorgeous. Drop-dead, too-handsome-for-his-own-good gorgeous.

"Wow." She didn't realize she'd spoken aloud until he smiled, the slow easy grin making her stomach flutter.

"Did you miss me?"

"How could I when you called me every day?" she whispered as Daniel and Melora took their seats.

"Well, *I* missed *you.*" His smile slipped away, his hands curving around her waist as he tugged her closer.

She went. Easily. Happily. Straight into his arms. He smelled of fresh air and aftershave, and everything she loved most in life, and she could have stayed there forever.

"How's the shoulder?"

"Better."

"I hear Chad is recovering, too."

"He has a longer road ahead of him, but they took him off the ventilator, and he's finally able to talk."

"Any memory of what happened?"

"None."

"We've been coming up blank, too. No fingerprints on the keys, no luck with the florists and so far all the Alamo Rangers have passed their polygraphs."

"Everyone agreed to test, right?"

"A few have been difficult to pin down. Anyone who hasn't tested yet isn't working today."

"Good." She glanced around, noting several familiar faces and a few that were missing

Soft music began to play as the memorial service began, and Levi leaned down, warm breath tickling her ear as he spoke.

"Go ahead and have a seat. I'm working outside for the next couple of hours. I'll be back as soon as I can." There he went again, with that melted-chocolate voice, and Susannah melted with it, her body leaning toward him, craving contact, longing for it.

His slow smile said he knew exactly what she was thinking, exactly what she was feeling, and her cheeks heated. "Go ahead. I wouldn't want to keep you from your job."

"See you in a few minutes." He grinned and walked away, leaving Susannah with nothing but her thoughts.

Was *see you in a few minutes* the same as *see you tomorrow?*

A half hour passed as a dozen people shared memories about Robert Riley. A minute of silence, and the group was dismissed to go to the garden for the opening ceremony.

Susannah filed out with the rest of the group, was just nearing the garden when a scream rent the air. Another scream followed the first, and Susannah raced toward the sound, following a half dozen Rangers who were converging on the Houston Gate.

They flung it open, spilling out into the street, and Susannah went with them, her heart stopping when she saw a man standing in the middle of the road, a woman held close to his side, a gun pressed to her temple.

"Open the border, Senator. Open the border, Mr. Vice President. Open the border, Governor Kingston. Open the border now! I demand it. The people demand it!" he shrieked, flailing the gun, his eyes wild.

"Sir, put down the gun. Release the woman." Levi approached from the left, his voice soothing and easy. If anyone could talk the guy out of murder, Levi could do it.

If anyone could.

If was the part that scared Susannah.

She sidled closer as Levi continued to speak in gentle tones. If she could just get close enough, she might be able to disarm the man.

"Stay put." Oliver Drew grabbed her arm, yanking her back, the force enough to jolt her wounded shoulder. The pain was intense, her eyes flooding with tears as she struggled to catch her breath, clear her thinking.

"No need to get rough," she whispered, and he scowled.

"Just trying to keep you from dying."

But she didn't plan to die. She planned to take a gun from a madman.

"Open the border. It is what the people want. Open the border!" The guy was becoming more frantic with every passing minute, his captive so pale Susannah thought she might fall over.

"Open the border." He swung the gun, pointed it at Susannah.

And that's when Levi lunged. One minute the guy was shouting his political views, the next he was face-planted on concrete, his protest soaking into the ground.

"Grab the gun, Oliver," Levi ordered, and Oliver Drew scooped it up, frowned down at it.

"It's not real."

"What?" Levi looked up, his eyes blazing.

"The gun isn't real."

"What kind of fool takes a stroll in front of police and Rangers carrying a fake pistol?" Levi growled, dragging the man to his feet and reading him his Miranda rights.

"They paid me to do this. They told me a fake gun would make no trouble," the guy babbled, tears streaming down his face.

"Who?" Levi frisked him, pulling a wad of cash and several rose petals from the man's pockets.

Bloodred rose petals.

Was *this* the guy who'd been stalking her?

She'd been sure it was someone she knew. An

Alamo Ranger gone bad, but the guy Levi was leading to a police cruiser was a stranger.

"The Lions. It is their job to open the border between Texas and Mexico. They hired me to help their cause. I meant no harm. Please, you must believe me. I meant no harm." He was still explaining as Levi helped him into the backseat of a squad car and slammed the door.

"Good job, bro! Looks like we've finally got our perp." Oliver patted Levi's back, his gaze following the cruiser as it pulled away from the curb.

"I'm not sure about that," Levi said, but Oliver shook his head.

"He mentioned the Lions. There's no mistaking that. He must be one of their low-ranking members." Daniel Riley scooped up the gun, tossed it into an evidence bag.

"It doesn't make sense. Why send threats if all he was going to do was come and shout political slogans? Why try to chase me off if he wasn't going to attempt to enter the compound? I don't think that's our guy." Susannah spoke as much to herself as anyone else.

"If you had a few more facts, you wouldn't say that." Oliver's smile didn't make his comment any less patronizing.

"What facts?" She lifted a rose petal that had

fallen to the ground, her skin crawling as she ran her finger over its velvety face.

"Nothing we can go into right now, and nothing you really need to worry about. Let's just hope he's the last guy who tries to interrupt. The speeches are scheduled to begin in ten minutes, and the planning committee doesn't want any interruptions." Oliver glanced at his watch, shoving his hat up on his forehead as he scanned the crowd.

"It would be nice if we always got what we hoped for, but since that isn't the way life works, I'm banking on the fact that our political activist isn't the last of the trouble we're going to see today." Ben Fritz scanned the still-stunned crowd, his face set in hard lines.

"A little action isn't such a bad thing. Especially since I came down from Austin for this gig." Another Ranger stopped beside Susannah, offering her a brief smile and a handshake. "Ranger Cade Jarvis."

"Nice to meet you. I'm—"

"Susannah Jorgenson. I've been hearing a lot about you."

"Hopefully good things."

"Would you want to know if they weren't?"

She laughed, and shook her head, wishing she felt as relaxed as the Rangers seemed to be. They moved across the road in unison, walking back through the gate. Daniel, Cade, Ben and Levi. Oliver. A fifth Ranger motioned for Susannah to walk through the gate, then closed it behind her. Like Daniel, he was vaguely familiar.

"How are you feeling, ma'am?"

"Better."

"Glad to hear it. We've been worried about you."

"Thank you, Ranger—"

"Anderson Michaels."

"You helped find the blue Mitsubishi."

"Right. Wish I could have found the guy who was in it. Maybe then you wouldn't have been shot."

"Susannah? Everything okay?" Levi strode toward her, his hair gleaming blue-black in the morning sun.

"I hope so."

"What do you mean?"

"I just don't think it's over."

"None of us do. We'll just stay vigilant. Keep our eyes open and pray." His arm slid around her waist, his warmth filling her as he walked her to the garden.

Keep her eyes open.

Stay vigilant.

Pray.

She could do all those things.

She would do them, because there was no way she believed that everything that happened over the ıst week had led to a fake gun and a few shouted ogans. Something bigger was brewing. She was ɜrtain of it.

NINETEEN

Something bigger turned out to be a whole lot
nothing, and as Susannah stepped through secu
rity at the Riverwalk Hotel, she wasn't sure if sh
should be relieved or concerned about that.

Something *should* have happened, somethin
well beyond a man waving a fake gun and shou
ing political slogans. But the memorial service wa
over, the speeches ended, the opening ceremon
complete and everyone was still alive and kickin
and ready for the luncheon hosted by the Alam
Planning Committee.

"Ms. Jorgenson? I'm glad you were able to mak
it to the luncheon." Hank Zarvy approached as sh
entered the ballroom, his broad face wreathed in
smile. "I want to be the first to congratulate you.
have to say, I had my doubts, but the security yo
put together for the opening ceremony was Texa
size perfection!"

"It was a team effort, Mr. Zarvy. I was only

ıall part of it." And she hadn't been any part of
e team during the ceremony, but she didn't men-
n that. The sooner Hank took his overly gregari-
s self off, the happier she'd be. She didn't like the
y. Hadn't liked him when they'd met at his house,
d his effusive praise wasn't going to change her
ind.

"Rest assured, your entire team will be rewarded
r their efforts. The Alamo Planning Committee is
ncerely grateful for the cooperation of the Alamo
ıngers during this event," he continued, appar-
tly not sensing her desperate desire to escape.

"I'm sure Chad will appreciate that. He's been
ncerned about the event and the fact that he'd be
spitalized during it. Having things go off without
ıitch may be the boost he needs to get him out of
e ICU."

"Let's hope that's the case. Looks like our guests
honor have arrived. Thank you again, Ms. Jor-
nson." He hurried toward the small group that
as being ushered toward the front of the ball-
om. Governor Kingston and his wife took their
aces at a large banquet table facing the room.
he lieutenant governor and his wife sat to their
ft. Senator Huffington took a seat to their right,
niling broadly as he surveyed the room, his wife
eside him. Everything looked just as it should,

and he was probably feeling as content and excit
about it as Zarvy.

Susannah just felt sick.

Deep-in-her-gut, worried-out-of-her-mind sick

"You don't look happy." Levi's dark-chocola
voice poured over her, but even that wasn't enou
to ease her anxiety.

"I just can't believe anyone would go to so mu
trouble and then…wimp out on the day of the eve
Two people were shot with a real gun, and then t
Lions send a man with a fake gun to interrupt t
ceremony?"

"Maybe security was too good. Maybe th
couldn't do more than that."

"You don't believe that any more than I do."

"You're right. I don't. Come on. I'll show you
our table. Then I've got to get back to patrol duty
The heat of his palm seeped through the thin lay
of her silk shirt, and she shivered in response.

"Cold?"

"Scared." Of what might go down, and of wh
she felt for Levi. He'd asked if she'd missed hi
and she had. Missed him with the kind of despe
ate need she was terrified to admit.

"You won't be hurt again, Susie. I promise yo
that." His words ruffled her hair, settled into h
heart, and she wanted to believe he had the pow
to fulfill them.

"I wish I could believe that," she whispered, and smiled gently as he pulled a chair out for her.

"You can. Enjoy lunch. Maybe afterward we can et some dessert somewhere quiet and talk about ings."

"Things?"

"You and me things." He turned away before she ould respond, striding across the room and disap-earing into the crowd, leaving her at the empty ble, staring at a dozen place settings.

Alone.

"Ladies and gentlemen, thank you for joining us r a celebration of all that is great about Texas!"

he crowd cheered as Rodney Tanner stepped up the microphone and began his opening speech, ut Susannah wasn't in the mood to clap and elebrate. She felt sealed in and cut off, alone with er worry and fear. The doors had been closed, Texas Ranger stationed at each one. Tall, short, old stars on their chests and on their belt buckles, ey looked capable of defending and protecting, ut that didn't ease Susannah's fear.

The door to the kitchen area swung open and everal waitstaff carried pitchers of water and iced a into the room. Susannah watched as they filled lasses, following their movements as they retreated ack into the kitchen. As the door swung open gain, she caught sight of the room beyond. Frantic eople preparing lunch. Texas Rangers watching.

A tall, lean figure appearing for a moment, pee ing out into the ballroom seconds before the doc closed.

Tall, lean, familiar.

Susannah's stomach churned, and she pushe away from the table.

"Going somewhere?" Oliver Drew asked, an she jumped, her heart leaping, then settling dow again.

"I just thought I'd see what was going on in th kitchen."

"Better not. It's crowded back there, and I don think they'd appreciate it." He smiled, but his eye were as cold and still as a snake's.

"Right. I'll give them space, then." She walke away, sure she could feel his frigid gaze drillin into her back as she hurried out of the ballroom.

There were half a dozen tall, lean men in th lobby. Another few in the corridor. Probably a mi lion of them in San Antonio.

But she couldn't shake the feeling that she kne the guy in the kitchen. Couldn't shake it no matte how many times she told herself to let it go.

A small exclusive restaurant enticed patrons t enter, and Susannah walked in, ignoring the hos ess and the shocked kitchen staff as she walked int the back.

"Ma'am, patrons aren't allowed back here. A round-faced chef approached, a frown creasin her brow.

"I'm helping with security for the VIP luncheon. 'e're checking all routes into the service area. 'oes your kitchen connect to it?" Susannah dug er ID out of her bag, flashing her Alamo Ranger adge. It wasn't much, but it looked official, and e woman seemed to buy it.

"Not directly, but there's a service hallway rough here." The chef led her to a door and pened it. "Just follow the sound of clinking lasses. They're preparing the champagne toast, nd then they'll serve the salad."

Susannah nodded, hurrying along the quiet hall-'ay.

A murmur of voices, the clink of glass against lass, the sounds drew her along the hallway to a ocked door.

Leave it alone, Susannah. Just turn around and o back before you make a fool of yourself.

She knew she should, but she'd come too far to urn back, and she knocked on the door, nearly fall-ng backward when it opened.

"Can I help you?" a tall, dark-eyed woman asked, nd Susannah fumbled for a response.

"I'm working with the security team." She lashed her badge as she had before and was sur-rised when the woman stepped to the side and let er in.

"Just stay out of the way, okay?"

"Sure." The room buzzed with activity, what

seemed like a hundred people preparing plate
filling pitchers, walking in and out of the swin
ing doors that led to the ballroom.

A hundred people, and not one of them was sli
and tall and familiar.

Had she imagined him?

She made a quick circuit of the room, pausin
near a door that led into another area. "Where do
this lead?"

"We gave your team the blueprints so w
wouldn't have to waste time explaining while w
tried to feed our guests," the woman snapped.

"Where does it lead?"

"Our wine room. They're preparing the cham
pagne there. Should be finished in a few minute
Better be."

"I'll check on their progress," Susannah said a
she opened the door and stepped into a dimly l
hallway. The sound of clinking glasses drifted o
the air, and she followed it, stepping into a cool dr
room lined with wine racks. Four carts of cham
pagne glasses stood in the center, several men an
women pouring champagne into them. They looke
up as Susannah approached, but didn't stop pour
ing.

Time was ticking by, and they must have felt
as acutely as Susannah did.

"Almost ready?" she asked, hoping she sounde
like she belonged there.

"Two minutes and we'll begin transporting, ıa'am." A handsome, dark-skinned man emptied is champagne bottle, set it down and opened an- ther.

"Good. Good."

"The VIP cart is being prepared next door. If ou'd like to check on that as well, feel free." He aid it as if she would know what he was talking bout, and Susannah decided to go with it.

"Sounds good. I'll do that."

"Just around that way. The door is at the back of ıe room." He gestured with his head, not breaking is rhythm, and Susannah walked around a rack of ine, found the closed door.

She hesitated with her hand on the doorknob, ıen pulled it open. A cart of champagne glasses at near the far wall, and a man stood facing it, is back to Susannah. Tall, slim, familiar, shov- ıg something into his pocket as he turned to face er.

"Susannah! What are you doing here?" Marcus's yes were wild, his face sallow. He looked as sick s Susannah felt.

"I could ask you the same thing, but I think I now."

"It's not what you think." He took a step forward, nd she put her hand up.

"Don't."

"Susannah, you don't understand. The hospital

bills are piling up, and I have debts. Big ones. The offered to pay everything if I did this."

"Who offered? What did they want you to do?

"Get the governor and lieutenant governor ou of the way, so that Senator Huffington could tak the governor's seat." He shrugged, acting for all th world like he wasn't talking about murder.

"You should have asked for help, Marcus. Yo know Chad and I would have done whatever wa necessary to pay off your debts."

"Typical Susannah response. True to the cours never wavering in your convictions. I actuall admire that, but it's not who I am. I've made mis takes. They've come back to haunt me. It's eithe do this, or my wife and child die. I don't have choice."

"There are always choices." She took a ste closer. She had to stop him. Had to.

"That's where you're wrong. There is no choice.

"Marcus—"

"I didn't want to hurt you. I hope you know tha I just needed you out of the way."

"What did you put in your pocket?" she asked but she knew. Poison. Which glasses had he poure it in? Who would die if Susannah didn't sto him?

"You should have stayed home. It would hav been better for both of us."

"You don't have to do this." She took anothe

step. One more and she'd be close enough to topple the cart.

"Yes. I do. I'm desperate. You don't know what it's like. You can't imagine."

"I can't let you do it."

"I don't think you can stop me." He lunged for her, and Susannah dodged, springing toward the cart, close, almost touching it before Marcus threw her back, his fist grazing her jaw.

"What's going on here?" The voice was familiar, and Susannah turned, expecting help, wanting to believe in it. She saw the gun as it swung toward her temple, felt a moment of blinding pain, and then she felt nothing at all.

TWENTY

Where was she?

Levi checked the hotel lobby for the fifth time in as many minutes, his pulse racing with an anxiety he couldn't shake. Something was wrong. Really wrong.

"Did you find her?" Daniel Riley asked, his gaze filled with concern.

"No."

"I had Melora check the restroom. She's not there. Maybe she got tired of this fancy shindig and went out for a hot dog."

"She would have let me know."

"You tried her cell phone?"

"Only a dozen times."

Where *was* she?

His phone rang, and he grabbed it, hoping to hear Susannah's voice. Desperate to hear it.

"Susannah?"

"Nope. Gisella. Sorry to disappoint you, but I think you'll forgive me when you hear my news."

"What news?" He knew he should care. She was at the hospital, after all, guarding their key witness. But all he could think about was Susannah and the empty spot she'd left at the table.

"Our guy is finally talking. Singing like a jay-bird, as a matter of fact. Says he was part of our favorite organization."

"The Lions of Texas?"

"Yep, pretty low-level guy, but moving up in the ranks. Would have kept on climbing, but they wanted him to be part of something he refused to do."

"Go on." He swung around, pacing back to the ballroom and waiting outside the door.

"They wanted him to apply for work at the Riv-erwalk Hotel. Wanted him to volunteer to work during this week's celebration, and they wanted him to help get rid of the governor and lieutenant governor during the luncheon. He wouldn't. Went to Pike with the information and the next thing he knew, he was waking up in the hospital."

"Does he know who the gunman was?"

"No."

"Too bad."

"Yeah, but he's convinced something is going down today. Says that Senator Huffington is will-ing to open the Mexican border, and the Lions want him in position to do that."

"Is Huffington a Lion?"

"Quin isn't sure, but he does have two names for us. You're going to love this." The sheer pleasure in her voice almost made him smile.

Almost.

"Who are they?"

"Hank Zarvy and Rodney Tanner. Quin says they're high-level Lions, and they're the ones trying to move Huffington into position."

"How?"

"Quin doesn't know, but the Lions *are* planning to act today, so you guys had better be on your toes."

"Have you told Ben?"

"He and Oliver are searching for Zarvy and Tanner. Ben said both men left the luncheon ten minutes ago. You're to stay on security duty. That's a direct order from him."

"Understood." Levi glanced at Daniel, saw his own excitement and concern reflected in the other man's eyes.

"Sounds like this luncheon might not be as boring as we expected." Daniel grinned, and Levi wished he were as enthusiastic.

"I need to find Susannah."

"You think she found out something she shouldn't have? Maybe walked into some trouble?"

"Knowing her, yeah." He opened the door, slipped into the ballroom, Daniel close on his heels.

The governor had taken his place at the podium,

and the guests were laughing as he regaled them with tales of a childhood spent reenacting the battle at the Alamo with his school buddies.

Cade Jarvis stood near the door to the kitchen. Levi motioned him over.

"Trouble?" Jarvis whispered.

"Plenty." Levi filled him in, shifting when Anderson Michaels arrived, making sure both men were fully informed.

"So, we have three missing persons. Susannah. Tanner. Zarvy. Only one is in real danger. How about Levi, Anderson and I search for Susannah? Riley, you want to find the captain and Oliver and help them round up a couple of Lions?" Cade asked as the doors swung open and carts of champagne were wheeled in.

"Brave men fought that day. Brave men died. Today, one hundred and seventy-five years after their sacrifice, we remember them still. Please, join me as we toast those mighty defenders, as we toast *all* of the brave men and women who have come after them, fighting for our freedoms and liberties." The governor's voice swelled.

The kitchen doors closed as the last cart was wheeled through, then flew open again, banging against the wall, a female figure sprinting out, running toward the VIP table.

A man dressed as a server raced after her, his dark eyes wide and worried.

"Don't drink it. It's been poisoned!" the woman screamed, throwing herself at the cart, slamming it into the wall, a million shards of crystal exploding into the air.

"Freeze!" Daniel shouted, drawing his weapon, pointing it at the intruder.

The dark-haired, freckle-faced intruder.

Susannah.

Blood poured from her head, staining her face, probably blinding her.

Don't move.

Do *not* move.

Levi willed Susannah to stay put, knowing one move would bring a barrage of bullets.

"Hold your fire!" he shouted, stepping between her and the guns pointed at her heart.

"Your lady sure knows how to make an entrance," Daniel said, grabbing a napkin from a table and handing it to Levi.

"What happened?" He wiped blood from her face, ignoring the comment. Ignoring everything but Susannah.

"Marcus. I thought I saw him. Found him downstairs with the champagne. The Lions paid him to poison it." Her eyes were glassy, blood still seeping from a deep gash in her temple.

"Call an ambulance," he shouted, but she shook her head.

"I'm okay. Listen. I saw him."

"Who?"

"The guy with the gun."

She wasn't making any sense, but Levi let her talk as he applied pressure to her wound. It was bad. Really bad.

"Is she okay?" The server who had followed her out of the kitchen held another napkin out to Levi. "I found her trussed up like a Christmas turkey where they were preparing the VIP glasses."

"I'm fine, but we have to—"

"What's she talking about? What gun? What poison?" The governor hovered a few feet away, his tux glittering with shards of crystal and wet with champagne.

"Cyanide." Despite the blood pouring from her head, Susannah was still on her feet and still talking. That was good. He hoped.

"In the champagne?" The governor looked dubious, but Levi didn't doubt Susannah's word.

"We need an evidence kit. We're going to need to test for poison," Levi said to Daniel, and he nodded, calling in the request.

"Levi..." Susannah swayed, clutching his arm to stay upright.

"You need to sit down."

"Oliver Drew."

"What?" He'd heard the name, though, felt it stab into his heart and stomach.

"He had the gun. Hit me with it."

"Are you sure?" He didn't want to believe it. Did *not* want to, but the truth of it was in Susannah's eyes.

"Yes."

"He and Ben are searching for Zarvy and Tanner together. Call Ben. Warn him." He turned to Daniel, saw that he was already on the radio.

"No response."

"We need to find them." But he couldn't leave Susannah. Couldn't walk away while her blood dripped onto the marble floor.

"Zarvy rented a hospitality suite on the third floor. We were supposed to have a drink there after the luncheon. Room 351. Could be you'll find them there," the governor spoke up, handing Levi a pass-key.

"Better go catch some bad guys, Levi, because I'll be really unhappy if a headache is all I have to show for my leap into the champagne glasses." Susannah stepped back, taking the napkin from his hand and pressing it against her wound, telling him without words that she'd be just fine.

"Come on, man. We don't want to lose another captain." Daniel's words broke the spell that held Levi in place, and he nodded, barking orders for two Rangers to stay with Susannah as he, Cade and Daniel ran from the ballroom.

They reached room 351 in tandem. Voices carried

hrough the closed door, and Levi shoved the card nto the door, waiting as the light flashed green.

Slowly, Daniel mouthed, and Levi nodded, easing he handle down, cracking the door open. Just a ectangle of light, a shadow beyond it.

"Go ahead and cuff them," Ben said, and Levi ealized he was the one blocking the light.

"I don't think so," Oliver responded, and Levi lidn't need to see his face to picture his arrogant smile.

"We don't have time for games, Drew. Cuff hem."

"Here's the thing, boss." He stretched out the last word. "Sometimes we Rangers catch the crook. Sometimes the crook gets away."

"Are you nuts? Put your weapon down." The anger in Ben's voice was unmistakable, and Levi cracked the door a little more, knowing that when he moved, it would have to be decisively.

"No. I'm just sick and tired of working for a salary that barely pays the bills. I want more, and he Lions can give me that. They made the offer. I accepted. It's just too bad that you and Greg got in my way."

"You killed Greg?"

"Today had to go off without a hitch. It's been in the works for years. With Huffington in line to take the governorship, all we had to do was get rid of the people who stood in his way. I knew when I got Greg's text message that he was going to rui that. I couldn't let it happen. Just like I can't let yo leave this room alive. The Lions of Texas are goin to roar. When they're done, we'll both be down You for good. Me with a flesh wound."

"Just like at the hospital." Ben shifted, and Lev caught a glimpse of a Ranger uniform. *Oliver.*

"A little poison taken the right way sure doe make a guy look innocent. Of course, if things ha worked out at the hospital, Quin would be dead."

Levi pulled his gun, waiting for just the righ moment, praying he'd know when that was.

"Take the gun, Zarvy. I know you've got th stomach for murder. Of course, if you kill *me* letter will be sent to every news organization i the state outlining the plot against the governor an naming you as conspirator. Make sure you don' kill me."

Now! Levi mouthed, slamming the door agains the wall as he threw himself into Oliver. Th Ranger went down with a huff of breath and shouted curse.

"It's about time. I was wondering when you' join the party," Ben grumbled, his gun pressed t Hank Zarvy's head.

"Hey, if you'd told anyone where you wer going..." Daniel cuffed Rodney Tanner, ignorin the man's sputtered protest.

"We can discuss that after they tell us what they

have planned for our lunch guests." Ben cuffed Zarvy, shoving him toward a couch.

"Poison in the champagne. A quick easy way to get rid of more than one person at a time. Fortunately, the champagne cart met a wall on the way to our VIPs." Levi dragged Oliver to his feet.

"And your girlfriend met the butt of a revolver. Sorry about that, but these things happen." Oliver shrugged and smiled.

"So do these." Levi pulled back his fist, stumbling backward when Ben dragged his arm down.

"He's not worth it."

"You're right. He's not." He nearly spit the words, slamming cuffs onto Oliver's wrists. "Have fun rotting, Drew."

He didn't look back, didn't bother explaining where he was going, just left the Lions and the Rangers. Left a man who should have been a comrade and friend.

Greg's killer.

He took the stairs, racing down two at a time and rushing out into the lobby.

"Levi! Over here," Corinna Pike called out, waving frantically from a small crowd that had formed near the ballroom. She looked small and delicate, her dancer's body clad in a flowing black dress, the gauzy sleeves splattered with what looked like blood. Melora Hudson stood beside her, her hair ruffled, her face pale.

"Are you two okay?"

"Is Ben?" Corinna grabbed his arm, her fingers cold through his shirt.

"Fine."

"Thank the Lord," she whispered. "I was trying to help the woman who was hurt. She just…collapsed. There was blood everywhere. Just like with my father." Her voice caught, and she raised a shaky hand to her mouth.

"We've caught his killer, Corinna."

Her eyes widened, her hand dropped away. "Who?"

"Oliver Drew."

"What!"

"Ben will explain. I need to find…"

"Clear a path, folks," an EMT boomed as he wheeled a stretcher out of the ballroom.

"Susannah." Levi ran with the ambulance crew, his pulse pounding painfully.

Susannah's pale, bloodstained face was still and empty as death.

"You coming?" the driver asked, and Levi nodded, flashing his badge and hoping they wouldn't try to keep him from riding to the hospital. No way would he leave Susannah again.

"Susie?" he shouted over the roar of sirens, his hand shaking as he touched her cheek. His body shaking.

Please, God. Let her be okay.

"Doubt she can hear you, buddy."

"How can I not with him screaming in my ear?" Susannah mumbled without opening her eyes.

"Can you open your eyes, ma'am?" The EMT leaned forward, flashing a penlight toward her eyes.

"I'd rather not." But she did, her eyes clear, emerald and not quite focused.

"Can you tell me your name?"

"Susannah Jorgenson. It's March 6. I got knocked over the head by a rogue Texas Ranger, and if Levi screams in my ear again, I won't be responsible for my actions." She closed her eyes, splotches of blood garish against her pallid skin.

"What if I whisper?" He leaned close, his lips brushing her ear, his pulse racing with desperation. He needed to keep her awake and talking and aware. If he didn't, she might slip away.

"Depends on what you say."

"What if I say you're the bravest most beautiful woman I've ever met?"

"I might tell you to keep talking." She opened her eyes, offered a weak smile.

"What if I say that the day you walked back into my life was the best day of my life?"

"I'd say that you must have had a pretty sorry life."

He laughed, his knuckles skimming her cheek, feeling warmth and life beneath her skin.

Feeling the future. A future shared with the woman he loved.

"Actually, Susannah, my life has been pretty good, but reconnecting with you…that's made it nearly perfect."

"You're a charmer, Levi McDonall, and you know what?" She grabbed his hand, pressed a kiss to his palm.

"What?"

"I think I just might like it."

He laughed again, the sound mixing with the scream of ambulance sirens filling the air, filling his heart as he and Susannah rode into the future together.

EPILOGUE

She'd been to a lot of weddings, but none was as perfect as this one. Susannah couldn't help smiling as the bride and groom exchanged a kiss. A love forged in difficulty and destined to last forever. She felt that as surely as she felt her own heartbeat.

The strains of the processional filled the Alamo chapel as the couple began their first walk together as husband and wife, Ben dashing in his tuxedo, his face glowing with love for his bride. Corinna breathtaking in a gauzy dress that hugged her figure. The bridal party followed. Gisella looking lovely in her bridesmaid dress, somehow outshining the other three attendants. The four men dressed in Texas Ranger garb were dashing, handsome.

"Beautiful. Just beautiful," Susannah breathed.

"The couple or the men?" Jennifer Rodgers, Anderson Michaels's fiancée, whispered as the bridal party followed Ben and Corinna down the aisle.

"I was talking about the couple, but I've got to

say, the men are spectacular," Susannah replied as Daniel Riley, Anderson Michaels, Cade Jarvis and Levi passed by, their black cowboy boots tapping on the floor.

They were all stunning, but Levi…

Levi eclipsed them all.

As if he sensed her thoughts, he turned and met her eyes, his face blazing with a love that left her breathless.

A love forged in difficulty.

Destined to last forever.

She'd been so afraid to believe in it. So afraid to trust that God really was working His plan and way through the troubled times.

But she wasn't afraid anymore. Not of the dark. Not of her nightmares. Not of the future that stretched out before them.

"Come on. We'd better go stake our claim before every woman at the wedding starts going after our men," Jennifer urged, and Susannah didn't have to be told twice. She hurried out of the chapel, walking past the old oak tree and into the Alamo gardens. Corinna and Ben had been given special permission to have their reception there.

Susannah paused at the entrance, inhaling the sweet spring air, watching as the couples she'd grown to know and love during the past few months paired off, hands twined, arms clasped, love glowing. Six couples formed through the struggle to find

Gregory Pike's murderer. Susannah hadn't known the man, but she thought he'd be pleased that his daughter and the Rangers he'd cared so deeply about had found happiness.

"You look beautiful." Levi walked toward her, his expression serious, his eyes scanning her face, and she smiled, reaching for his hand, pulling him closer.

"So do you."

"I'm not sure that's a compliment." He frowned, and she laughed.

"It is."

"Then I accept. So, why are you standing here by yourself?" His fingers threaded through her hair, his touch light, but more compelling than any other man's had ever been.

"I just want to drink this day in, memorize it, so when tough times come, I can remember how God blessed so many people during such trying circumstances."

"You know what I want to remember?" He pulled her close, looked down into her face.

"What?"

"How you look right now. In that blue dress with your hair falling all around your shoulders."

"Remember when you told me we'd come full circle? Friends. Then not friends. Then friends again?"

"Yes."

"I think the Rangers of Company D have come full circle, too." She shifted, turning in his arms so they were both facing the reception area.

"Yeah?"

"You've all made peace with your losses. Moved forward with your lives. Found what you were looking for."

"I think you're right, Susie. Proving that Senator Huffington was a member of the Lions of Texas was the final piece of the puzzle."

"The events leading up to that were definitely a time of discovery. Rodney Tanner, Hank Zarvy and Oliver Drew are going to be tried for murder, attempted murder, and drug trafficking. Marcus has already pleaded guilty to attempted murder and assault. Quin Morton is recovered and serving as a witness for the prosecution. The Lions of Texas have been destroyed, their organization scattered, their drug trade stopped."

"But it's not all we've discovered," Levi said.

"I know that Huffington was a Lion, but there's no proof he had any knowledge about the plot to kill—"

"That's not what I'm talking about."

"No?"

"I'm talking about what we discovered when we looked into each other's eyes that first night at the Alamo. That we'd never really lost each other. That we'd always been part of each other's hearts."

"And always will be," she whispered, standing n tiptoe, pressing a kiss to his lips.

"Break it up, you two. We've got a picture to ake," Gisella Hernandez called out, and Levi oked into Susannah's eyes.

"Ready?"

"For what?"

"Pictures."

"I'm not in the wedding party.'

"This isn't going to be a wedding party photo."

"No?" She let him tug her toward a small group athering in the center of the garden.

"It's a photo of the members of Company D and f the people they love. I thought we'd hang it on he wall in our living room."

"*Our* living room?" She stopped, not sure she'd eard correctly.

"Ours. I think this fall would be a great time r a wedding." He pulled a jeweler's box from his ocket, and her heart leaped, her mouth went dry.

"You can't do this here. It's Corinna and Ben's vedding, and it's just—"

"Perfect!" Corinna called out.

"I talked to them about it a month ago. They greed that, after all we'd all been through together, his would be the best place to tell you how much I ve you. How desperate I am to share my life with ou."

"Desperate?"

"I don't know any other way to be when it come to you." He smiled, opening the box, pulling out ring.

A beautiful ring that she could barely see throug her tears.

"So, what do you say, Susannah? Will you marr me?"

"Say yes!" someone shouted.

"She'd better. If she doesn't, he'll never live i down," someone else responded.

Daniel. Susannah was almost sure of it, and sh turned to look. Saw all of them standing together Daniel and Melora. Gisella and Brock. Anderso and Jennifer. Cade and Paige.

Ben and Corinna.

Love forged through trial and through pain Love built on shared experience, founded on trust steeped in faith.

Love like the love she shared with Levi.

She turned back to him, her hand shaking as sh held it out, her heart soaring as she met his eyes saw his love for her there.

And then she did exactly what everyone was beg ging her to do.

She said yes.

* * * * *

)ear Reader,

\fter struggling to recover from a brutal attack, \lamo Ranger Susannah Jorgenson is clinging to ıer faith and doing her best to get her life back. Iaunted by the past, she faces every day with trepidation. When she'd asked to serve as the head of ecurity at the opening ceremony of the Alamo's 75th anniversary celebration, she knows it's her ast chance to prove she can continue to do the ɔb she'd always loved. As Susannah works with hildhood friend Texas Ranger Levi McDonall, she ɜarns that the most difficult trials often lead to the nost profound blessings.

I hope you enjoy reading the last book in the 'exas Ranger Justice series as much as I've enjoyed vriting it. I love to hear from my readers. You can 'isit me at shirlee-mccoy.blogspot.com or drop me line at Shirlee@shirleemccoy.com.

3lessings,
'hirlee McCoy

QUESTIONS FOR DISCUSSION

1. Susannah is honored to be chosen as head of security for the opening of the Alamo's 175th anniversary celebration, but she's worried about her job as an Alamo Ranger. Why?

2. She knows she's going to be working closely with the Texas Rangers, but has no idea that she'll be working with Levi. What are her thoughts when she sees him for the first time?

3. Levi has fond memories of Susannah. Even when they were kids, he wanted to protect her. What impact does that have on his work relationship with her?

4. Susannah feels the need to prove that she can continue her work as an Alamo Ranger, but she's worried that her fear will keep her from doing her job. What character traits keep Susannah working despite her fear?

5. Do you see those traits as strengths or weaknesses?

6. How does Susannah's past affect her relationship with Levi?

7. Why is she hesitant to share with him what she's been through?

8. Does knowing about Susannah's past trauma change Levi's feelings about her? Why or why not?

9. Levi feels that he failed Greg Pike by not getting to his house in time to save him. Do you think this makes him more protective of Susannah?

0. Levi has a job to do, but he can't deny the attraction he feels for Susannah. How well is he able to balance his personal and professional interests?

1. Susannah knows that God has never abandoned her, but she does mourn her past and the changes it brought to her life. Have you been through experiences that have changed you in very deep and fundamental ways?

2. How have you come to terms with those changes?

3. The most difficult times in our lives often teach us the most valuable lessons. What lessons have Levi and Susannah learned through their experiences?

14. How does learning those lessons bring ther closer to God and to each other?

15. Did you suspect who Greg's killer was, or wa it a surprise?

LARGER-PRINT BOOKS!

GET 2 FREE LARGER-PRINT NOVELS PLUS 2 FREE MYSTERY GIFTS

Love Inspired® SUSPENSE
RIVETING INSPIRATIONAL ROMANCE

Larger-print novels are now available...

YES! Please send me 2 FREE LARGER-PRINT Love Inspired® Suspense novels and my 2 FREE mystery gifts (gifts are worth about $10). After receiving them, if I don't wish to receive any more books, I can return the shipping statement marked "cancel". If I don't cancel, I will receive 4 brand-new novels every month and be billed just $4.74 per book in the U.S. or $5.24 per book in Canada. That's a saving of at least 24% off the cover price. It's quite a bargain! Shipping and handling is just 50¢ per book in the U.S. and 75¢ per book in Canada.* I understand that accepting the 2 free books and gifts places me under no obligation to buy anything. I can always return a shipment and cancel at any time. Even if I never buy another book, the two free books and gifts are mine to keep forever.

110/310 IDN FC7L

Name (PLEASE PRINT)

Address Apt. #

City State/Prov. Zip/Postal Code

Signature (if under 18, a parent or guardian must sign)

Mail to the **Reader Service:**
IN U.S.A.: P.O. Box 1867, Buffalo, NY 14240-1867
IN CANADA: P.O. Box 609, Fort Erie, Ontario L2A 5X3

Not valid for current subscribers to Love Inspired Suspense larger-print books.

Are you a current subscriber to Love Inspired Suspense books and want to receive the larger-print edition?
Call 1-800-873-8635 or visit www.ReaderService.com.

* Terms and prices subject to change without notice. Prices do not include applicable taxes. Sales tax applicable in N.Y. Canadian residents will be charged applicable taxes. Offer not valid in Quebec. This offer is limited to one order per household. All orders subject to credit approval. Credit or debit balances in a customer's account(s) may be offset by any other outstanding balance owed by or to the customer. Please allow 4 to 6 weeks for delivery. Offer available while quantities last.

Your Privacy—The Reader Service is committed to protecting your privacy. Our Privacy Policy is available online at www.ReaderService.com or upon request from the Reader Service.

We make a portion of our mailing list available to reputable third parties that offer products we believe may interest you. If you prefer that we not exchange your name with third parties, or if you wish to clarify or modify your communication preferences, please visit us at www.ReaderService.com/consumerschoice or write to us at Reader Service Preference Service, P.O. Box 9062, Buffalo, NY 14269. Include your complete name and address.

LISUSLP11

LARGER-PRINT BOOKS!

GET 2 FREE LARGER-PRINT NOVELS PLUS 2 FREE MYSTERY GIFTS

Love Inspired®

Larger-print novels are now available...

YES! Please send me 2 FREE LARGER-PRINT Love Inspired® novels and my 2 FREE mystery gifts (gifts are worth about $10). After receiving them, if I don't wish to receive any more books, I can return the shipping statement marked "cancel". If I don't cancel, I will receive 6 brand-new novels every month and be billed just $4.74 per book in the U.S. or $5.24 per book in Canada. That's a saving of at least 24% off the cover price. It's quite a bargain! Shipping and handling is just 50¢ per book in the U.S. and 75¢ per book in Canada.* I understand that accepting the 2 free books and gifts places me under no obligation to buy anything. I can always return a shipment and cancel at any time. Even if I never buy another book, the two free books and gifts are mine to keep forever.

122/322 IDN FC79

Name (PLEASE PRINT)

Address Apt. #

City State/Prov. Zip/Postal Code

Signature (if under 18, a parent or guardian must sign)

Mail to the **Reader Service:**

IN U.S.A.: P.O. Box 1867, Buffalo, NY 14240-1867

IN CANADA: P.O. Box 609, Fort Erie, Ontario L2A 5X3

Not valid to current subscribers to Love Inspired Larger-Print books.

Are you a current subscriber to Love Inspired books and want to receive the larger-print edition? Call 1-800-873-8635 or visit www.ReaderService.com.

* Terms and prices subject to change without notice. Prices do not include applicable taxes. Sales tax applicable in N.Y. Canadian residents will be charged applicable taxes. Offer not valid in Quebec. This offer is limited to one order per household. All orders subject to credit approval. Credit or debit balances in a customer's account(s) may be offset by any other outstanding balance owed by or to the customer. Please allow 4 to 6 weeks for delivery. Offer available while quantities last.

Your Privacy—The Reader Service is committed to protecting your privacy. Our Privacy Policy is available online at www.ReaderService.com or upon request from the Reader Service.

We make a portion of our mailing list available to reputable third parties that offer products we believe may interest you. If you prefer that we not exchange your name with third parties, or if you wish to clarify or modify your communication preferences, please visit us at www.ReaderService.com/consumerschoice or write to us at Reader Service Preference Service, P.O. Box 9062, Buffalo, NY 14269. Include your complete name and address.

LILPI1

ReaderService.com

You can now manage your account online!

- Review your order history
- Manage your payments
- Update your address

We've redesigned the Reader Service website just for you.

Now you can:

- Read excerpts
- Respond to mailings and special monthly offers
- Learn about new series available to you

Visit us today:

www.ReaderService.com

RS10